RUIN

Rebecca Jaremko Bromwich

DEMETER

Ruin
Rebecca Jaremko Bromwich

Copyright © 2022 Demeter Press

Demeter Press
PO Box 197
Toronto, Ontario
Canada
K0L 1P0
Tel: (905) 775-9089
Email: info@demeterpress.org
Website: www.demeterpress.org

Demeter Press logo based on the sculpture "Demeter" by Maria-Luise Bodirsky
www.keramik-atelier.bodirsky.de

Printed and Bound in Canada

Front cover image: Rebecca Jaremko Bromwich
Front cover artwork: Michelle Pirovich
Typesetting: Michelle Pirovich

Library and Archives Canada Cataloguing in Publication
Title: Ruin / by Rebecca Jaremko Bromwich.
Names: Bromwich, Rebecca, author.
Identifiers: Canadiana 20220169586 | ISBN 9781772584097 (softcover)
Subjects: LCGFT: Novels.
Classification: LCC PS8603.R645 R85 2022 | DDC C813/.6—dc23

Guinevere

Very little grows on jagged rock.
Be ground. Be crumbled.
So wild flowers will come up
Where you are.
You have been stony for too many years.
Try something different. Surrender...
Where there is ruin, there is hope for treasure.
—Rumi

The long, broad boardroom table was dark, glossy oak with a high sheen. Beige walls with impressionist art, interspersed with large windows, surrounded the table. Enid's black Chanel blazer brushed across the smooth surface of the table as she gestured with her right arm and, at the same time, flicked the switch on the clicker to advance the slide presentation. She smiled. "Equality," she said. "Substantive equality. It means equity. It means ensuring opportunities and inclusion for everyone fairly. Let's talk about it. How can we work together towards this? For example, how can we best facilitate access to justice through our firm's pro bono program?"

Around the long table, the group of grey-suited white men, the few white women smattered amongst them, and the one Black man, leaned forwards, waiting for her next sentence. Behind them, through the windows, a spectacular view of Canada's parliament buildings, tall in their light brown gothic elegance, with their green roofs, could be seen in the distance under a grey spring sky. On the wall behind them was an elegant black and white photograph of a seashell, a labyrinthine spiral spinning majestically against a linen background.

Enid paused, revelling in the moment, still feeling a small thrill to have their attention, to have the opportunity to speak to them, to work with these smart people, to collaborate on their team, and to be working, again, as a lawyer. She had come a long way from her prairie childhood and from her days as a Cincinnati housewife. She was glad of both the destination and the journey. Before she left Canada for Cincinnati as Arthur's trailing spouse, she had worked as a crown attorney in Ottawa. She'd left that behind for many reasons and no longer wanted to practice criminal law. She didn't want to be on either side, didn't want to put anyone in jail or to try to keep them out. Enid had wanted to find somewhere to work as a lawyer in the space between the polarities of guilt and innocence, somewhere that she could contribute differently. Now, back in Ottawa, she worked at a large law firm, focusing on its pro bono, or community service, efforts. She was grateful to be again half of the power couple that she and her husband Arthur, who was a surgeon, were seen as. She sometimes felt like an empress in her suburban kitchen, much as, in her office, she felt humbled by the great professionals surrounding her. In her community she felt intimidated by the wealthy women there, as though she might at any point be exposed as any number of imperfect things, as though her flaws might show—her PTSD, her eating disorder, from which she was recovering, her difficult youth, her brush with criminality. Outside the window, a gull flew across a grey sky, the path of its flight arching across the parliament buildings and the Ottawa River in the distance.

Enid's iPhone shook in her pocket. She glanced down at it furtively, seeing only the date: March 10, 2020.

When her presentation was over, she read the text.

It was from Morgana. "Mom, Daddy declawed the cat."

"What?" Enid said out loud to no one in particular. Shaken out of her feeling of general contentment, she felt sick. She sat heavily down in her chair, sinking down from where she had been standing at her standing desk. She hastily dialed Morgana's number.

Morgana was crying. "Mommy," she said, sounding much younger than her thirteen years, "I don't know if Artemis will make it. She seems..." Morgana sobbed, "sad."

Artemis was a smooth, slender black cat who had been their constant companion since their days in Cincinnati. She was older now and had always been an indoor cat who tried to escape when possible. But, lately, with Enid and the kids all out of the house during the day, Artemis had taken to escaping through windows, developing a vigorous determination to hunt.

"I'm coming home," Enid said. "It will be okay."

"No it won't mom, and it's your fault."

"My fault? You said *Daddy* declawed the cat."

"Your fault she got out again. Because you weren't home where you should be, because you went back to work, not caring about the house at all. You don't care about us. It is ALL YOUR FAULT." Morgana was crying.

Even with Morgana's tears, Enid was not going to let that last comment go. "Morgana, I am sorry this happened, but it is not about *fault*. I am a person, and I have every right to have a job. Yes, my work is important to me but so are you and your sisters and your brother—and the cat. I am sure your dad says those things to you, but surely you can judge for yourself."

There was a dial tone on the other end. Morgana had hung up.

Her children's emergence into their teens had been tough for Enid as a parent. Wolfgang, at fourteen, was not so tough, mostly just loud and a bit smelly but with a wonderful sense of humour and a kind, kind heart. However, her daughters, Morgana, Freya, and Sybil, and Lenore were now teens. The twins Morgana and Freya were seventeen, Sybil was fifteen, and Lenore, thirteen—which was challenging and sometimes resulted in mother-daughter conflicts, and that was tough, particularly as they'd had close relationships throughout their childhoods. Enid knew the girls needed to assert their individual personalities. Their conflict with her was normal development. Her son, Wolfgang, on the other hand. didn't glower or yell at her as much, but she was worried about him. When he'd been a small boy, he didn't tell her when his hands were cold. She'd been shocked, running warm water over his tiny fingers, how cold he had gotten without saying a word. Enid was worried that underneath Wolfie's humour and silences, there might be sadness, or something else he was hiding.

Enid felt sick to her stomach about the cat and also about what Morgana had said. Morgana was angry. Angry teenagers are cruel and selfish, but they are not necessarily wrong. Enid knew she had, for a long time, found herself emotionally distracted, numbed to some degree by depression after she'd found out about her husband's online flirtations and as his distance from her grew. She'd been preoccupied by anxiety in her attachment to him, and it had been hard for her to focus on her kids' needs. Be the parent they needed. She'd felt them slipping away, not just because they were teens but also, she increasingly acknowledged, because Arthur controlled all major decisions and did not support her authority with the kids. It was as though he somehow couldn't understand her as a separate adult, and he approached problems as though he was the only one trying to solve them. Enid figured it was fair she should acknowledge she struggled with a team approach to parenting too. Because the kids were his too, and she was struggling with that. He had been quite absent for much of their childhood, perpetually travelling or at work, and Enid wrestled to recognize the legitimacy of his opinions about the children.

Enid got ready to leave her office at 4:00 p.m., earlier than she usually left but not egregiously so. Morgana needed her. Enid could hear it in her daughter's voice. Enid felt hot as she closed her laptop and slid it into her briefcase, heading out the door. Declawing Artemis was something Arthur had threatened for a long time, and he'd put the onus on Enid and the children to keep her inside "or else," but she hadn't gotten out lately; she'd been less antsy about getting outside in the cold of winter. Declawing Artemis now seemed—vindictive. Enid felt, gnawingly in the back of her neck, that she should have seen it coming. Artemis had been hunting again, escaping when the screen door swung open. She had been leaving her prizes in the living room, and Arthur couldn't handle the mess.

Enid drove her black, late model Lincoln Nautilus east from downtown Ottawa to her home in the tiny nearby suburb of Rockcliffe Park. It was a spacious, white and black Tudor-style house on Hillsdale Road that overlooked Sand Pit's Lake, otherwise known as McKay Pond, a posh spring-fed lake that had once been a gravel pit and was now a haven for swimmers and blue herons in summer. Arthur had done well for himself financially here as he had in Cincinnati, and Enid and the children lived comfortably on his salary, largely in his absence. Sometimes Enid had dreams about her house sinking into the ruins of the gravel pit beneath. This was part of her ongoing PTSD.

When Enid walked in the door, Freya was holding Artemis. Arthur was not home. Artemis was floppy, looking groggy. Her front paws were bandaged.

"What did the vet say? Enid asked, taking Artemis into her arms and holding her smooth, silky frame close. She could feel Artemis's heart beating against her chest.

"The vet?" asked Freya.

"The vet who declawed the cat," Enid said.

"Mom," said Sybil, standing in the kitchen doorway, "there wasn't a vet. Daddy did it himself."

Now Enid could feel her own heart pounding against her chest.

"What?"

"He took her to the hospital this morning," said Morgana, "to the operating room." Morgana was crying again. She threw her glass into the sink. It shattered. She was bleeding. Enid walked over to her and helped her rinse her hand, then wrapped it with a dishcloth. Fortunately it was only a small amount of blood, and Morgana was not badly hurt.

Enid went to her room, put her briefcase down, and crumbled onto her bed. She was so angry with Arthur but needed to calm down before she spoke to him. She knew he would throw her emotion back at her if she wasn't perfectly calm. She phoned her mother, Judith Alger, who lived in Alberta.

"Mom," she said, "how are you?"

"I'm fine, just fine," said Judith brightly. She was home now, again, after another period of time in mental health care. Enid had not seen her in several months, but she did sound well.

"How are you?" Judith said, happy to hear from her daughter.

Enid felt tears on her face. She started to tell her mother what had happened, started to say Arthur's name, and wanted to tell her mother about the cat. But she thought better of it. She did not want to upset her mom. She composed herself just saying, "I'm well. Kids are well. Looking forward to travelling to Europe this summer."

"I always thought I would like it there, but remember when we went to Paris? I hated it. So crowded and dirty."

"Mom, you must have liked it a little—the desserts and the Eiffel Tower."

"Not really. Guess you can take a girl out of Alberta, but you can't take Alberta out of the girl. It's part of me. Can't take away what's part of me."

"I hear you," Enid said, cradling the phone with one hand while she stroked Artemis's head with the other, visualizing the big sky over the tiny white bungalow she had shared with Judith when she was growing up, the postwar bungalow near Nose Hill Park in the north end of Calgary, Alberta. The glittering lights of the skyline, the dry, prairie wind, the scent of the grasses, all of those things were part of her too.

"Arthur and I are going out tonight, so I have to get ready. I'll call you again soon, Mom. I'm so happy that you are feeling well again."

"Bye Eenie dear. Talk to you soon."

Enid closed her eyes. She had to get ready to go out later, but she needed a nap. Soon she was dreaming. It was the same nightmare that always haunted her, since her car accident when she was a teenager.

The car kept rolling. How many times, Enid didn't know. But when it finally stopped, her head and shoulders were outside the driver's window. She woke up drenched in sweat, her heart pounding.

Forty-eight-year-old Enid Kimble got her bearings, glancing around her room. Her breathing slowed as she realized she'd once again awakened from the nightmare.

It was March in Ottawa, Ontario. This dream, this nightmare, always took place thousands of miles away, near Okotoks Rock, a famous glacial erratic in Alberta. The rock, sacred to the Niitsitapi, also known as the Blackfoot or Blackfeet, the nation of Indigenous people whose territories straddle the Alberta-Montana border, the southern border of the prairie province in Western Canada where Enid had lived in her childhood. The rock was there, with its petroglyphs, its ancient writings, standing strong. Enid had always been fascinated by the Okotoks rock, which had broken off from a mountain chain.

Now in her dream, she saw her mother's vibrant red hair dancing in a chinook, frost on prairie grass, a young man with wavy hair and a dangerous smile, the Okotoks petroglyphs, a white stag, and a car spinning out of control and rolling, rolling, rolling. But this time, as she had not for several years now, not since she lived in Cincinnati, she also saw her five children, and that dimension of nightmare sickened her with its return.

Enid had woken up with her poor cat still lying injured in her arms, as her children stood around her crying. She felt dizzy, thinking of the movement that had made all the mountains—not just the castaway rock but the chain itself. Slowly sitting up, Enid was thinking of how those mountains surged up from the ground in tectonic plate activity. The world was not a place of stillness with one wreck contrasting against it. No, the geological world was always in flux, unstable, molten at its core. And Arthur was not who she had thought he was. She didn't think he had this cruel streak in him, or maybe she hadn't let herself think it.

Now she was ready to speak to him, so she called his private office number.

"You declawed my cat?"

Arthur sighed his customary, curt, dismissive sigh. "I performed a simple procedure, an onychectomy, to protect our furniture. An elegant solution if I do say so myself. The animal was a pest. It's better off this way."

"Arthur, you operated on our cat in a children's hospital?"

"Sure," he replied, sounding smugly well pleased with himself. "Anaesthetic works the same. A cat's not so different from a baby."

"No, not so different from a baby at all." Enid took a deep breath, enraged now. "You are a fucking psycho. You sliced up our cat! You took pieces of her. That's cruelty to animals, Arthur. You amputated the last bone of each of her toes. That's like cutting off each of your fingers at the last knuckle. It is an unnecessary surgery that provides no medical benefit to the cat. Not to mention, Arthur, cats need to hunt. It's what cats do. Maybe I should cut off your fingers, your surgical instruments, so you understand."

"There you go again," said Arthur, "shrieking and being irrational." He paused and went on, icily, "You'd better calm down and not be late for my award presentation tonight. The show must go on, Enid. Maybe take a Percocet. Those help settle you in these...emotional episodes." He hung up.

Enid slammed down the phone. She calmed down, hugged her children, and walked out into the night, down the path behind the house to the pond. She had not taken a Percocet from the pill bottle Arthur had prescribed her. Instead she lit a cigarette and stood by the water, contemplating jumping into the icy lake. It would not drown her, likely. It seemed like a refreshing suggestion, plunging out of this pleasant, apparent idyll, this new vacant, beige Elysium Arthur had been able to provide for them, no longer in the American Midwest, but now in Canada, into clean, cold water. Enid wanted something to change; she wanted out. She snuffed out her cigarette, thinking of her children, went back inside the house, showered, and changed. She hugged each of her children tightly as she left for the evening with Arthur.

Enid was a bit surprised at how effortless it was for her to smile politely and applaud that evening at the cocktail reception, but, then again, she had been the background to Arthur's foreground for a long time. She found herself wishing he would trip over the cords on his way to the microphone. No such luck. Arthur never stumbled, at least not in ways that others could see.

"True greatness," said Arthur, referring to himself, flashing a grin from the podium, his bonded teeth glinting in the floodlights onstage, "requires courage. And teamwork. Like the moon landing. We must continue to be brave."

Enid usually cringed at the eye rolls in the room when Arthur spoke this smugly, but tonight she enjoyed them. That, she thought, must be what Arthur thinks eyes look like. Even so, she nodded and smiled, clapping at points he emphasized. As she often had, Enid felt like a magician's assistant, all sequins and heels, directing awe at the performer and then hiding in a box somewhere uncomfortably, only for the audience, to, when she reappears after a gymnastic effort, applaud the magician.

In the car, on the way home, smoothing her black dress as she sat in Arthur's Tesla with rain pounding on the windshield, Enid said, "You know, there are lots of stories about Guinevere. So many variations."

"Oh Christ," said Arthur, his hands on the steering wheel, looking straight ahead. "Here we go again with a mythology lesson. Enid, do you never get tired of extraneous information about fiction told by anonymous dead people? You don't have a single congratulatory word to say about my achievement? I worked hard for this. Many hours. Many lives were saved. I'm kind of," he said, without a hint of irony, "a big deal."

Enid said, "Sure, yes, you saved lives, and I can't argue with that, but you've never acknowledged that I've supported you, or frankly, that a whole team supports you all of the time, and if you are on their team, you are supposed to support them. And if you are on my team, you are also supposed to support me." A tear slid down her hot cheek. "Even in the most ancient texts, Guinevere gets her own story arc. Sometimes she's kidnapped by Mordred; sometimes she runs away with Lancelot; sometimes she goes to a nunnery. There are so many versions of the story about Guinevere," she said again. "But she always, always leaves Arthur. There is always a Guinevere after Arthur, after Camelot."

Enid wiped the tear away. "And," she said, feeling her heart pounding in her chest under the necklace she had been given for her wedding. "In the end," she said, pausing for effect.

"In the end, who the hell cares what happens to that spoiled princess, after Guinevere lacks a larger vision, gets self-absorbed, loses focus, and lets the kingdom fall?" asked Arthur, glancing over as he pulled the car into their driveway.

Enid glanced over at him and smiled, opening the door. "He can blame her if he wants, but in the end, Arthur's kingdom lies in ruin." She slammed the door and ran quickly inside the house out of the rain, not looking back at Arthur, who was still in the car.

"Maybe," she heard Arthur's voice call after her. "Maybe I want to burn it down."

She heard him back up and saw the headlights of his Tesla move on the door as he spun off. By the time she looked back, he was gone.

She didn't know where he'd gone, and at this moment, she didn't really care.

Lockdown

Two days later, the whirring conversations of global civilization became a sentence that for a least a time trailed off into silence. On March 13, 2020, the entire country of Canada locked down, as did much of the rest of the world. This meant people could not leave their homes except for emergencies, and no one quite knew how a terrifying disease was spreading, let alone knew how to prevent its spread—when schools and offices were closed and everyone who could was working and studying from home. The COVID-19 pandemic halted life for Enid, for her children, and even for Arthur, in unprecedented ways.

The ruin of Enid's hope for a happy marriage emerged as obvious in the midst of that COVID-19 pandemic of 2020, in the mess of a muddy, slushy March, and of ongoing renovations. Her law school friends who worked in family law pointed out that she was not alone—their businesses were booming. A lot of marriages, it turned out, couldn't withstand so much togetherness. Enid and Arthur's "dream house" was under construction after several years of occupancy while it had been in an imperfect state. The ruin of the marriage had been submerged for a long time beneath the momentum of their busyness. Arthur was renovating the house frenetically, as he worked tirelessly as a surgeon and in business too. It had been a source of amusement and frustration when they'd lived for four months with no kitchen, but that had been a year before and not during a lockdown. Now peripheral to their day to day, as Enid was home with her kids home from school, the renovations continued endlessly as Arthur also continued to head to the hospital daily, as though he were trying to correct things.

Arthur, whom Enid had met at Queen's University, where both had attended professional schools, had, as she had imagined he would do when she first met him, become a successful surgeon. But that was never enough. He lied about his height. He lied about his income, exaggerating it. He was still blonde, although there were now some grey flecks in his hair. He was tall, but not quite as tall as he pretended, with excruciatingly exact posture. Arthur told their friends he was "democratizing health care" through his work. He was a brilliant innovator and talented surgeon. He was alarmingly calm in crisis, took risks, moved quickly, and was daring. But online "rate your doctors" reviews also said he was arrogant. Also that he flirted with his female patients. Enid told him about that last one, and he had the website delete it. Arthur never laughed out loud. He would just smile and make the motions of laughter silently. He told jokes but was not one to laugh at jokes told by other people.

The fabric of their marriage had frayed. Most of all it was because Enid didn't like him anymore, even though she still loved him in some way.

He drove a Tesla with white seats

"Who the hell has five kids and buys a car with white seats?" Enid asked, when he brought it home.

"They will just have to keep it clean," shrugged Arthur about the car, not looking up at her but rather down at his phone.

Arthur exaggerated when he told stories, "How is it less of a good story if it isn't true?" he said when Enid rolled her eyes about it.

"Authenticity," Enid said. "People crave authenticity."

"People?" said Arthur, wryly, still gazing instead down at his phone.

"Who are you texting" Enid asked, sighing, because she had said it so many times that it felt like a mantra.

"The hospital," muttered Arthur, absently, walking away. "Work."

Enid was left standing in their elegant kitchen, red dishcloth in hand, as he walked away.

"Arthur," she yelled, following him. "Maybe you could avoid exaggerating if the story has me in it... and I'm right there." She flung the dishcloth at the wall. It landed with a slurping sound, leaving a trail of water on the wall as it slid to the floor. "I'm tired of being trapped in your grandiose narratives. Canada may even survive for ten minutes without the intervention of you!!"

Arthur looked up now. His hand was on his office door. "Enid," he said, "I am a crucial player in the solution."

Enid laughed. "I would like it if you were a more crucial player in the care of your five children. You have a savior complex without a hint of irony, Dr. Kimble."

Arthur sighed. "Maybe I'm tired of being trapped in your storyline too." He stepped into his study and closed the door.

Enid stood there for a minute, hands on hips, then heading back to the kitchen, leaned over, and picked up the dishcloth. She walked back to Arthur's office, balled the wet cloth up and threw it, hard, against the closed door. He did not reopen it. A framed wedding picture fell off the wall though, and the glass smashed.

Enid did not pick up the picture. It was a beautiful photograph of a picture-perfect love story. In order to be beautiful, stories don't have to be true. Enid tried the handle to his office door. It was locked. She banged on it. "You declawed the cat, Arthur, damn you. That's cruel. That's what you did to her, to Artemis, and to me. You want to declaw me too. You are a terrible fucking husband, Arthur. I hate you." Enid started sobbing loudly.

Now, Arthur opened the door. "If you are the cat?" said Arthur, rigidly, not losing the calm tone in his voice, "Who the hell says you are the cat? Declawed? Fixed? Maybe I am the goddamn cat. I can't get a drink, can't go to a meeting after work, without you blowing up my phone, Enid. I have fifteen minutes of free time a day and it's during my commute." He paused. "Maybe I just don't want a cat."

He closed his door again.

"You are right, Arthur. You are in the wrong fucking story. I don't want you in mine."

*

Arthur, it is true, was a hero in the wrong story. There is a story to be told about him saving lives, slicing cancer out of children's throats, helping democratize healthcare access in the Global South. That story was true. But it was not Enid's story to tell. And, right now, he was the absolute fucking villain in her story.

Enid looked up the hall and saw three of her five children standing in the doorway to the kitchen.

"Mom," said Wolf, his eyes teary, "stop!"

"Leave Daddy alone," hissed Morgana. "You ruin everything."

Sybil was crying.

Freya was out with Lenore in the garden and had heard the argument. She came in, "Mom, I think you and Dad make rhyming versions of the same mistakes."

Was it possible to love someone and have it not turn into captivity? Could two people love one another and not feel trapped? In straining too hard to control and contain the other, both Enid and Arthur had failed and lost what they were fighting to attain. And maybe, Enid hoped, that was the insight to be gained: We don't have control over it. Both wanted to be free but paradoxically both had tried in their way to domesticate the other. Enid wanted to stop feeling like an imposter in this supposedly happy marriage. She was tired of living in this borrowed shell—the shell of the hermit crab.

They'd agreed that the kids would travel back and forth after Enid got her own house. With Artemis. A house downtown, by the canal, in need of repair. For Enid, the first lockdown was a series of blurred days marked by how much her nail polish had chipped off. Cold days, blustery, early spring. Finally, after three weeks, she stopped counting the days and removed the polish in its entirety. All of her shallow, rich white lady daily joys—her nail polish, Pilates classes, lunches with friends, even work at an office—were all taken from her now. It was hard not to be sad about having the mundane pleasures of her life ripped from her, and she had to acknowledge that she was grieving for her lost way of life but had to put that behind the knowledge that people were dying. Enid had tried to work, from her laptop, as the kids whirled around her, and they attempted, like so many around them, to enjoy various spirit-raising lockdown activities, like making sourdough bread, playing board games, and watching the *Tiger King* train-wreck documentary. Nothing seemed to happen except for the snow slowly melting around them, a melt that signified time passing when nothing else, anymore, did.

Now it was the other rooms, in Enid's new home, that construction workers banged around in every day, refinishing hardwood, building cubbies, repainting walls, adding an extension here, a deck there.

Elora Frank, Enid's oldest friend in Ottawa, came by for a walk. "Your old place reminds me of Boldt Castle now, or even the Taj Mahal," she said—Grandiose ass epic gifts from husband to wife never to be completed, or at least never to be given to the fucking wife."

"Yes, I guess," Enid said. "In both of those historical examples, the wife died. In this case, it looks like the story is ending with divorce. So, Arthur and I are finished with the marriage. I'm renovating my new house, but there is another renovation to my life. Nothing is ever enough for Arthur. And here I am." Her voice breaking, Enid continued, "At the end of our journey together, the end of our marriage, still relatively young, and not sure where to go next."

"Enid," said Elora, "I'm sorry." She and Enid hugged. "You want to hear this right now, I know, so I will tell you: Arthur is an asshat. What you maybe don't want to realize is that he's always been a fuckstick asshat. And Enid Alger is a bad bitch. You are. You still are. Thank fucking God you won't be wasting any more time on his skinny ass."

Enid laughed and cried and said, "But the kids... I'm going to keep trying."

"Fuck him, Enid. Why try? He is just a bringer of misery."

"But the kids."

"You know what, Enid," said Elora, "here's a random fact that resonates right now. There is another castle in the Thousand Islands, near Boldt Castle, but it's not a ruin. It's called Singer Castle. The dude who built it had an empire of sewing machines, stitching things together. And their family lived in it for generations. Now it's a hotel. Locals call it the Lucky Castle. Hang on to this vision: It is possible to build things. Not everything ends up in ruin."

The months wore on. Spring warmed slowly into summer, and the quarantine measures were lifted somewhat. They could eat outdoors again, and some activities resumed. Yet every day was, as they joked, "blurrsday." One day slid into the next with time, and their lives became suspended in a kind of bewildering limbo, in which it was unclear when, if, or how the world could start up again.

Labyrinth

Enid decided she would begin her journey out of divorce at a wellness retreat near Bancroft, Ontario, called Grail Springs. It was in fact Enid's favourite yoga and wellness retreat, located on a small, pristine lake, called Chalice Lake, in what locals call "mountainous country." For Enid, who had grown up in the shadow of the Rockies, they looked like hills, but they were beautiful. Mineral deposits ran rich through them, producing interesting rock formations. Enid had discovered it in 2016, shortly after they returned to Canada.

Last time she was there, when the marriage was just crumbling but had not disintegrated—when she went through the labyrinth, the walking maze at Grail Springs, she saw a black cat on the way out, and went to pet it—it felt like a sign. It looked so much like Spanx, the cat she had been torn up about losing when she was in hospital recovering from the car accident she'd had when she was nineteen. This time, when she went into the labyrinth, someone had tied a diamond engagement ring with a white ribbon on the crystal rock in the middle. Enid saw that as a sign too.

When you enter the labyrinth, you are supposed to bring your troubles, spiral in with them, and then you leave them behind on the way out, walking the circuit that you need to walk to do that. You walk into a maze to get lost and into a labyrinth to be found. This sign of the ring was clear to Enid: Leave the marriage behind and walk away from it. Time to let it go. It was then that Enid resolved to go to the jeweler to have her diamond rings remade into a tennis bracelet. Her husband had asked her to let him go, and she would do that. She would stop living in that borrowed shell.

The journey into divorce started much earlier, of course, Enid thought as she was walking. It was hard to track it back. Maybe it started before their wedding, when Arthur's mother picked his wedding band, and Enid marched to the jewellery store to pick a different one, and Arthur seemed confused about the fact Enid wanted to choose it. Maybe it started with the classes they went to together with the officiating minister before marriage, when the minister shook his head at their compatibility scores and told them that there were some important differences. They laughed at the time, but his last name was Omen, and his wife left him the morning before he officiated at their wedding.

Maybe it started when they had their first fight before they got married. It had been about whether Enid should take on her husband's name after marriage. He'd insisted, rigidly, that she should, even though it was not what Enid wanted to do. That sense of foreboding she'd felt about his cool, controlled insistence on his way had grown over time. There'd been a nagging feeling all along that the whole thing wasn't quite real, in retrospect. There was a sense that Enid didn't quite know Arthur Fulbright Kimble the Third very well after all. That he was not solid enough to hold on to. Like he dissolved when not visible. As though he didn't quite exist.

Certainly, they were on the path to divorce by the time their marriage counsellor told her, in a parting one-on-one session, "Enid, he doesn't care what you want. He does not care what you want." Maybe it was the path they were on all along—to some extent they'd agree on this. They had both wanted a family; they had wanted kids. They had wanted a home. He was a smart man and witty. Enid enjoyed the banter they had together. He was going to medical school; she was going to law school. They were a power couple. The résumés matched. But, in the end, there is a difference between passion and hiring. Their careers matched, but they didn't.

After having been really on her own since she was eighteen, and even sporadically before, Enid had wanted someone stable to take care of her, a soft place to land, a respite. She had wanted a family, a Norman Rockwell family, and Arthur promised and delivered on that—at least, to all appearances. But Arthur was fastidious, exacting, emotionally absent, and impatient with any kind of mess.

The funny thing about that, Enid thought after a Google search, was that even Norman Rockwell did not have a Norman Rockwell family. His art was always an aspirational, creative fiction, which does a kind of violence against the imperfections of reality. Wikipedia says that Norman Rockwell was married three times. His second wife committed suicide. He was notoriously obsessed with his work and controlling.

Enid sighed. The price of a utopian vision is high. The price of perfection is ruthless rage when there is a mess. If you find yourself in

Elysium—Enid thought as she had a few years ago, in her pleasant suburban retreat in Cincinnati—you are dead.

They had come back to Canada, not because Enid had wanted to, even though she did, but because Arthur had been offered a job. It had been a happy coincidence. Now, Enid was able to work again as a lawyer, which she was happily doing. It had also given Arthur a chance to reconnect with people from his past, too, and he had really reconnected with one of them. Quite closely in fact.

Enid had relinquished a lot of control in exchange for the stability marriage to Arthur offered— the cover. She had loved him. She was hard pressed to say what she loved about him. He was successful, intelligent, and the father of her children. Beyond that, they didn't have a lot in common.

She wasn't the one who'd initiated the divorce because she figured they could work on accommodating each other. In reality, in the whole arc of their marriage, Enid wasn't the one who had initiated anything. It was a one-sided accommodation all along. They had lived in the house he picked, named the kids the names he picked, drove the car he chose, and hung the paintings where he wanted them. When Enid had selected the occasional holiday destination, he was outraged and sulked for weeks. So, intellectually, she knew by the time it happened, that the parting was for the best. But she'd been so emotionally attached to him. At Grail Springs retreat, a Buddhist teacher had Enid and her friend Bella pick up rocks for an exercise, carry them around all day, and mindfully pour their energy into them, with the intention of putting them down the next day. The teacher then said, "See? It's hard now, isn't it, to put the rocks down? You have grown attached to the rocks." And that was a really good point: Attachment is something we hold on to, not necessarily something the object of attachment earns or deserves. We can grow attached to a rock.

The process out of the relationship was going to be a process, Enid realized, of learning how to dream her own dreams, envision her own future. Emerging from the ruin of her marriage was going to have to be a constructive journey: She knew she had to learn how to build a future for her kids and herself, on her own. She had to stop borrowing that shell— like a hermit crab does to protect itself. She had to learn to survive to show them survival was possible. And for her own sake too.

If there is historical depth, there are ruins. We live atop ruins all the time: in physical geography, and in our lives, at least by the time we hit midlife. Or by the time midlife hits us. Midlife had hit Enid like a Mack truck. Her allegedly devoted husband, whom she had married when she was twenty-three and he was twenty-five, had decided that he just didn't want to be married anymore when he was about forty-six. This was an issue, since he was married, and he had five kids. It took about four more years for Arthur and Enid to disentangle and finally separate. Really, it took the pause that COVID-19 imposed to break their momentum.

It was at the end of that summer of 2020 that Enid decided to go to the jewelry store on Bank Street in the Glebe, a neighbourhood in Ottawa. Her mistake was going to hot yoga before heading to the jewellery store to have the diamonds in her rings repurposed into a bracelet and sell the gold. The engagement ring and anniversary ring slid off easily, but the wedding band was stuck. The lady behind the counter said she had the option of using a contraption that would cut the circulation to her finger, and trying to squeeze the wedding ring off, or to cut it. She looked up at the woman and knew immediately how she wanted to proceed. "Slice it." she said, her gaze level, her voice low. Then she smiled, a little sheepishly, "I guess it is obvious that I am getting a divorce?" Her smile was, of course, obscured by the cloth mask she was wearing, the masks they were all wearing, because of the COVID-19 pandemic. It was a helluva time to be alive. They laughed. A man came from the back with a battery-powered device that looked a bit like a drill. Enid had to hold still as it started whirring, grasped on to the ring. "It's a thick ring," he said, "a strong one." After a moment, tiny sprinkles of gold dust fell onto Enid's fingers.

"Yes," she said, "like a handcuff. Keep working at it."

It seemed like forever passed as Enid sat there, eyes glued to the ring, until there was a click. She felt numb, and was dry eyed, registering that this was an upsetting event that she, at some point, might find herself upset about. He pried it open. And, it sat there, a ruin, like a piece of art or an archaeological artifact—a ring, sliced through, its symbolic gold circle of eternity broken, wrecked and ruined.

"Can I take a picture?" Enid asked. She felt empty but also free.

The jeweler and the clerk nodded. They may have smiled. It was impossible to tell because of the masks.

Enid texted the picture of the broken ring to Arthur with the message: "I am gone."

Enid decided she needed to travel. But how in a pandemic? She needed to create a new narrative, and she decided on a travelogue – through the ruins of a marriage, and through the ruins of various societies around the world. During the course of their twenty-five-year marriage, she had taken on the role of primary caregiver to the kids, and her career took a backseat to her husband's work as a surgeon, tech innovator, and doctor doing medical outreach in the Global South

He worked, travelled, and worked some more, and Enid did the legal work for his medical company for its first five years. During that time, it went from existing in their basement and on a website, until it grew into an actual thing in the world with around one hundred employees and an office building. Then, it was acquired by a German company, and, as a result, around the time Enid's husband decided Artemis needed de-clawing, he also became rich. Correction: They became rich.

Greatly to Arthur's chagrin, it was, legally, Enid's money too. He'd made the mistake of marrying a lawyer. She'd always joked, even on their wedding night, that divorcing her would be "very expensive," and she hadn't lied. So Enid ended up, at forty-eight, finding herself in the ruins of the life she had tried to build with Arthur, the ruins of their plans and dreams. She was feeling like she was sitting atop the prow of a wrecked ship that was broken and singing. She was trying to excavate herself— Enid Alger, whom she'd buried beneath their union, whom she'd hidden away when they moved to Cincinnati, when she had decided to run away from her legal career and her culpability for her past and when she decided to be like the hermit crab and hide in a shell that was not hers.

Enid had gradually become aware of how this situation had translated into Arthur's dominance within their marriage. She felt herself trying to salvage her children's best interests from the descent of the hulking wreck. She'd envisioned them all there in a little lifeboat, tossed onto a stormy sea. Except they were teenagers, and distress manifested as rage. And, in the midst of all this, shortly after Enid left, Arthur's twenty-three-year-old girlfriend made an appearance.

Enid had always been a helluva survivor. She had, as a teen and young woman, survived a car wreck, a miscarriage, her mother's breakdown, her move far from home, and, ultimately, law school. She'd always been determined to be a survivor, not a victim, and, after surviving, to be something else, not defined by the experience of trauma or difficulty or adversity—to be her best self.

In the divorce settlement, Arthur proposed to care for the kids half of the time. Enid was skeptical of that at first, but ultimately accepted it. Fighting it would be a losing battle. And there was an upside. Enid was suddenly promised some free time. So she decided to take a journey, to have the physical journey mirror her internal shift somehow. Enid had always loved world mythology. As an undergraduate, she had studied anthropology and archaeology. She had dreamed of travelling the world doing development work and research. A particular region of interest for her had been the Inca Empire, and she had, for years, dreamed of travelling the Inca trail in Peru. She'd studied Spanish in the hope of being able to live there. Before she left for law school, living mostly alone in the bungalow she shared with her mother Judith, because of Judith's hospitalizations, her most expensive possession was a wall hanging made of Alpaca wool, woven by Quechua people living near Machu Picchu. Instead of going there, though, Enid went to law school and got married to Arthur, whom she met during the first week of class. But she had always hoped to get to Peru. Towards the end of their marriage, Arthur, ironically, or Enid had sometimes thought viciously, went to Peru three times, travelling with his colleagues, and, it turned out, the woman who was already his young girlfriend while he was still married to Enid, on development work, trips on which Enid was not invited. He told Enid was going to Lima, but he lied. He went to Machu Picchu with his twenty-something girlfriend.

When Enid was a girl wandering solo on the streets of cold-winter Calgary, a different kind of labyrinth, she had this fantasy about walking with someone. She had written a poem about it, about walking beside a life partner, "walking forever to nowhere over rain-soaked streets." And she had thought Arthur was that partner, but he never really looked like the shadow of her dream. And he never really walked beside her, not after the first couple of months. He walked ahead. He was never one to make much eye contact. But, at some point, he must have loved her. There were relics of that around her, artifacts: the box he made her; the painting of manatees he brought her from a trip somewhere, maybe Florida; her wedding ring, too, which she had sliced now. She didn't know if the right answer was for her to travel alone for a while, and it must be, but she also didn't want to give up on the prospect of attachment, of walking with someone, of having a travelling companion on the remainder of life's journey.

Maybe she knew the marriage had ended that day in March when he declawed the cat. Or when the pandemic made it harder for him to conceal his extracurricular relationships. Or earlier. Enid thought perhaps it had ended in October of 2018, when she was alone with the kids and he was travelling and she needed help, and she cried to her friend Elora on the phone that she was burning out, and Arthur didn't take her calls because he was "too busy." She had been alone in a hotel room with all five kids having just given a talk, with them in the body of the lecture hall, for lack of childcare, having driven them down to Queen's University with her, and he was too busy, last-minute travelling, hanging out with friends to bother to be supportive on the phone. And Queen's was important, as it was where they had gone to together, where they had met, and she had realized, on driving by Arthur's old residence, and going to the pebbled beach with the kids, that he had moved on and left her behind.

And, maybe, really, it had ended that afternoon on October 2, 2014, in Cincinnati, when Enid told Arthur she wanted to go back to the law, when she finally set the wheels in motion to return to her career. He had, in retrospect, seemed to feel betrayed by that. And maybe he was. That nagging feeling that had first itched at Enid—that something about their relationship was not quite true—had overcome her that day, and she had never quite felt the same about him afterwards.

Maybe, none of those things were particularly significant, and the ending of their marriage was simply inevitable. Maybe they were each walking another labyrinth through their own lives. and this was just a step in their journeys, which would make sense in retrospect, and one day they would say it just had to be that way.

New Birth

Enid was leaving their family home. She'd bought a new one, but, meanwhile, she planned a journey through ruins, a year of wandering through the ruins of the world's ambitions as a way to sit with her own feelings of loss. Canadian law requires one year of separation before a legal, "no-fault" divorce, and neither she nor Arthur had an interest in trying to make a legal case for this being the other one's fault. So it would take a year to end things. Enid decided to make the narrative of that year a travelogue, and in that year, she planned to journey through the ruins of a marriage towards divorce, and a travelogue across continents: Europe, North America, Asia, South America, and back to Europe. She intended it also to be a year of journeying through meditation and yoga and through renewed energy and involvement in her children's lives. It was an ambitious agenda, and one doomed to be altered by the ongoing COVID-19 pandemic. Very little of her planned travel would be possible.

Enid's wedding ring became a ruin, an artifact. Her wedding photos and family photos with them as spouses together became artifacts too. As a forty-eight-year-old mom of four teens and tweens, Enid was inspired by Cheryl Strayed and her journey to the Pacific Coast Trail, leading to her book *Wild*, and by Elizabeth Gilbert's book, *Eat, Pray, Love*. Enid wanted to take a journey to find herself. However, with all that was going on in her home and in the world, she didn't have the time, funds, luxury, or otherwise have the ability to just take off for an extended period, so she settled instead on a planned series of relatively brief journeys, to see great monuments and wonders of the world—in short, to see ruins. The trips planned were Greek Islands, Everest Base Camp in Nepal, Galapagos Islands in Ecuador, Machu Picchu in Peru, and, finally, to wrap up the year, the Camino de Santiago, a trek through Spain that people on spiritual quests have been making for centuries.

Or that was the plan. It was meant to be *Eat, Pray, Love, North: A Canadian Middle-Class Woman's Voyage through Midlife to Self-Discovery and Empowerment*. But COVID-19 continued, and travel became a fantasy, or a forbidden dream, and the whole middle-class world she and Arthur had been living in— the world of kids' activities, and dinners in restaurants, and trips to Caribbean resorts, and concerts, and baseball games—all of it shrivelled and disappeared into dust with the pandemic lockdowns and restrictions. The busyness of Arthur, all of his travel, and the kids' lives, and their commitments, all spiralled into a confusing mess. And Enid didn't like disorder in terms of time. It was overwhelming.

Enid wanted to clear her head, to get a new perspective on how humanity can live atop ruins, among them, and survive and thrive, to find purpose amid all of this evidence of purpose misspent, or wasted, or defeated. She wanted to find a way to be in the driver's seat and to be herself.

In the course of Enid's marriage, she had moved to four different places in support of Arthur's career. She had to reinvent herself and restart her career in a different area of law in each of them. This was not without joys, and Enid learned many skills, especially flexibility, in the process. But she was always accommodating him, and then the children, always putting their needs first. She pursued a PhD in the last place they lived, and she became a professor for a while before she went back to a law firm, wanting to do what she had dreamed of doing, at least as a lawyer.

Enid was very glad she had five children, whom she loved desperately, and caring for them had been the central preoccupation of her life. It was a lot of work, which she mostly did on her own. But her husband said he wanted to separate, announcing it on their twenty-five anniversary, after dinner. He didn't say that exactly, but said he had ordered a bed to temporarily move downstairs and that he wanted to have 50 per cent time with the kids, which Enid supported in principle, but doubted was possible given his work schedule.

She decided, after weeks of tears, to leverage the separation as an opportunity, to have the chance to travel to the places she had wanted to go before, as the Robert Frost poem said. The road she had taken turned into a way that led to another way, and she could not turn back, and fortune placed her in large and comfortable suburban homes in a range of North American cities.

Actually, she decided to do this at Grail Springs, the yoga and meditation retreat she'd visited, after speaking to some women there who had walked the Camino de Santiago. And she had sort of started on this journey a year before when she booked a trip for her and Arthur, with the kids, to Kenya, in the hopes that her husband would start to understand their children as potential travelling companions instead of burdens to leave behind. This did not work. He was angry about the cost of the trip.

So, in 2018, Enid had been to few places: a brief backpacking trip through Europe in 1998 that her husband came along on, some resort trips "down south," visits to his family in the UK, and a short trip to Paris when he had a conference there, but not many. She resolved, when the separation started in earnest, to travel the world one or two weeks at a time. This plan was complicated by COVID-19, as it started in 2020, but Enid was able to plan the following itinerary. In fall 2020, She booked a trip to Naxos to see ruins, and to Santorini, in Greece, near the centre of the ancient, apparently matriarchal, Minoan empire. In January 2021, she had a yoga retreat planned in Florida. In May 2021, she planned to go to the Everest Base Camp and spend time in the heartland of Buddhism. Enid fantasized about the prayer flags, whipping in the wind with a backdrop of the Himalayas, mountains that would be both strange and familiar as she had grown up in the shadow of the Rockies. In July 2021, she planned to go to the Galapagos, and then at last to Machu Picchu. In October 2021, she intended to walk the Camino Santiago to Finisterre, which the people who travelled that pilgrimage in the medieval period thought was the edge of the earth.

On her glassed-in back patio, sitting on a stone seat overlooking the stillness of the Rockcliffe Pond, Enid planned her journey. Her children were playing cards in the living room of the house behind her, and she enjoyed the sounds of their laughter and occasional arguments as she sipped the chamomile tea that reminded her of her mother, Judith. Enid closed her eyes to savour the moment. She wanted to relish the sounds of her children's voices. Somehow she wanted to freeze in her mind the view from the house she would soon be leaving behind, hoping she could create a space of safety and peace for her children elsewhere. Enid knew, with a sharp pain of sadness, that this would always be their childhood home, that they would always go back here in their minds, as she would, that nothing she could build for them could replace that. She would have to make something new.

There had been times, definitely, when Enid's marriage to Arthur was a good one. Enid had to remember they had had a good run for a while.

When they had gone for drinks in Cincinnati, she had liked the way his eyes crinkled at the corners. She had been charmed by his stories of surgical shock and awe. They had experienced the births of their children together, with, admittedly, Enid doing the heavy lifting. Nonetheless, Arthur had held her hand, and he had been doing lifting of his own. Enid had loved him, really, truly, even if there had never been the sparks she had felt with others. But it had been a long time, by the time the pandemic hit, since he had been supportive of her. And the pandemic forced the issue. Arthur, usually always absent, was suddenly around. That didn't go well. Even so, even at their best, he didn't really see or take an interest in her soul in the way she would have hoped a partner would: She had always been expected to be the supporting act, the woman behind the man, the magician's assistant, Guinevere to Arthur, and there are some women, many women, who would have accepted that, if not been happy with it, but it was never what Enid had wanted. She had wanted to be a writer, a lawyer, an archaeologist. She had wanted to be Indiana Jones and James Bond. In short, Enid wanted adventures, and in particular, adventures of her own.

Enid exhaled slowly, trying to shake her attachment to the house, focusing on the illustration of attachment that the Buddhist teacher had asked everyone at Grail Springs to understand by carrying around a rock: We can get attached to a rock. It was not the rock, then, that was special, but our relationship to it—the way we reach out into the world and ask for it to embrace us back, something more about ourselves than about the things themselves that we reach out to.

"Shit," Enid said softly to herself, "is getting real." It was raining lightly, and it was cold and dark in the morning. The summer and its changes seem hectic and increasingly far away. The change to their lives is solidifying into reality, and tomorrow she would move.

She would leave this kingdom she and Arthur had built together, as Guinevere left Camelot, as she had left Calgary on a Greyhound bus. Enid knew about herself that she could survive but was thinking about the ruins she would leave behind, about how her children would be living amidst the ruins of her marriage: their home, or their part-time home, would be like an archaeological site, with family photos still in situ, to be taken down by Arthur at some point—no longer reflections of a living set of meanings but mirrors, artifacts, relics, ruins, objects belonging not to the present but to the past.

October

"*October is about trees revealing colors they've hidden all year. People have an October as well.*"

—Jim Storm

In October, Enid and Arthur had been physically separated for six months and started the legal processes towards finalizing a divorce settlement. Enid had not initiated the divorce, but once they were into the period of separation, she badly wanted to move through it to the final divorce.

They had a four-way meeting, via Zoom, with their lawyers. And now, Enid decided to make her way to Athens, in the midst of a pandemic, doing something controversial and perhaps crazy in its own way, but mental health is important, and if the risk of this mission to heal her mental health would be death, Enid, actually, would choose death. In the past few years, married to Arthur, she had been, at times, suicidal anyway. That is the truth. Now Enid was no longer suicidal. She was reaching forwards into the possibilities of the future. She needed to find a sense of hope in order to come home and parent her children.

Enid wanted to embrace the future, but she was not ready to rebuild. She resolved to travel around the world: Europe, Asia, and then South America to look at ruins. To sit with ruins. To sit in the sadness and the sense of loss she felt, to grieve the future she thought she had, the love she thought she had found. She resolved to carry that sadness with her around the world and leave little pieces of it everywhere and let the places she went fill her up with hope and promise, and knowledge, or at least something other than this sense of failure and rootlessness. She resolved to leave the shell of herself, the one like a hermit crab, behind her.

Enid's friend Elora Frank drove her to the Ottawa airport in the rain. Elora was a criminal defense lawyer who worked with her now elderly uncle, Joe Frank, at the firm Frank and Frank LLP. They'd been friends since Enid's days as a crown attorney, before she had kids and left Ottawa. Elora had black, long, curly hair, tidy red-shellac fingernails, and always wore black boots. She had grown up in Scarborough, in a tiny subdivision on the eastern edge of Toronto, near the escarpment bluffs overlooking Lake Ontario, and had a brash freshness that Enid loved. She also dropped F bombs on a regular basis, turning profanity into an art. They wore masks in the car, as dictated by COVID-19 protocols, less because either of them was nervous about the disease or particularly interested in following rules than because they didn't want to be delayed by a police stop. The disease was so strange and seemed unreal to both of them. Being stopped by the cops long enough to miss a plane, however, was a risk they both understood. Elora's mask said, "Fuck around and find out." Enid's was one of the disposable surgical masks Arthur had brought home from the hospital.

"So I've got this case that makes me think of you, Enid," said Elora as they blasted through the empty streets along Airport Parkway, away from Ottawa's city centre. "An 18-year-old girl is charged with careless driving, not causing bodily harm. The allegation is that she stopped for a deer, to let it cross the road, and get this, a cop car ploughs into the back of her. It turns out that the girl is six months out of being a crown ward, and she was driving a borrowed car from some creepy-ass older boyfriend. He wasn't there. Anyways, the charging officer has this real hard on to see her punished, and the Crown screening on the file says they will be asking for six months in jail." The Crown screening was an initial review that prosecutors made of files when they handed over disclosure of the case against an accused to the defence lawyer, where the prosecution indicated what sort of sentence they would be asking for from the court in the matter.

"Oh! It's like that Quebec woman who stopped for ducks. The one who ended up killing someone?" Enid said. "She went to jail. But here, no one died though, and it's Ontario. Guess it's a s. 130 Highway Traffic Act case? A POA case? That's pretty small potatoes for a senior counsel like you, Ms. Frank." A POA case was a case under the Provincial Offences Act, a regulatory infraction, by definition less serious than a Criminal Code case, and, as a result, not something people would usually pay much money to a lawyer about and generally not something the prosecution would look for jail time for breach of. "Why does the Crown want the highest possible sentence?"

"You tell me, Enid, I never know what those fuckers are on about. You're the one who used to be one... well, alright. She has this record for a bunch of assaults in group homes. You know, teens bitch slapping teens and then bullshit charges. But they make her look bad. It's her first adult matter, but there's a legal aid certificate because the Crown wants jail time. I want to see her acquitted."

"You're not going to plead her out?"

"Hell no. She has a defence. She could have been avoiding the deer to protect herself." Elora looked over at Enid, "Anyway Officer Dumbass hit her from behind. Rear-ended her. At fault, presumptively, uptight ass looking muthafucker, badge or no badge. It made me think of you, since you told me about what you got away with in Alberta as a teen: the accident. And how you so badly wanted a chance to plead guilty. Fuck that shit, Enid. None of your accountability restorative justice crap. You needed a fighting chance, and you got one. I want this girl to get away. She needs a fighting chance."

Elora said, as she pulled into the airport, "Remember, Enid: On your trip: hook up, but don't get stuck. Sure, men are fun to fuck, but the men are not the plot."

"Elora," laughed Enid, "Surely some are actually human, even if Arthur isn't. My son is a human being."

"I will give you that. Little Wolfie is a sweetheart. But men, I'm not so sure about in general."

"Joe's a human being. Your uncle Joe is a sweetheart."

"Yes. That's two. That's exactly two demonstrably valuable men. And one future potential in Wolfie there. Out of four fucking billion. Fuck, there might be even five or ten more. Sounds like your dad is okay. Atticus seems like an alright guy. That leaves us with very, very poor odds of finding another decent man out there."

"Come on, Elora! Have a little hope! And Martin Ginsburg. There was also Martin Ginsburg. Total ally and partner to Ruth Bader Ginsburg."

"Hope? Martin Ginsburg is an outlier, an exception to the rule. One supportive man in the history of woman lawyers is not statistically significant." snorted Elora. "Being single is the hope. I wasn't married as long as you. Only five years. But it was long e-fucking-nough. He kicked the shit out of me enough times for it to be enough."

"I'm sorry, Elora... I know that must have been terrible."

"Yeah, it was unmitigated shit. But I pulled myself out of it—a long time ago." Elora said brightly. "And, anyways, Arthur is also an unmitigated shit. He just pulled his stunts more surreptitiously. Too sophisticated to kick the shit out of you literally. He did it figuratively. Insidiously. Fucker never had a car seat in his car—with five kids. And wasn't he a no-show for prenatal class?"

"He came to the first session, and then didn't come back. He was busy," Enid said, weakly repeating what she had so often said, "as a surgeon."

"Oh fuck whatever, busy and important that asshat. It was his baby. Wasn't he busy seeing patients on the floor half an hour after you gave birth? And when Morgana had surgery last year? Didn't he pull the same exact shit when she was in the OR—go see patients and not sit with you? There are other staff at the hospital, you know. Motherfucker could call someone to cover his shit for a couple hours. Lord knows he does it when he travels as white saviour surgeon in the third world."

"He was there for the actual birth, and the actual surgery, but right after... he was busy."

"Such a bucket of bullshit. I've been saying it for years, haven't I, to divorce his ass? Glad it's finally happening. He can eat shit."

They pulled up to the departures lane at the deserted airport, where Elora's red Miata was the only car.

Enid said. "If Arthur calls you..." she started.

Elora snorted and tossed her long, curly black tresses haughtily. "I wish the muthafucka would. I have so much advice to share with him. About all the things he can stick right up his pale pink clenched, prissy poncy faux-British ass."

Elora parked. They both stepped out of the car and stood behind it. Elora opened the trunk, and Enid pulled out her suitcase. As she did, her cigarettes slid out from her purse onto the cement.

Elora leaned over and picked them up. "What the fuck is this?"

"I think that's obvious,"

"They're fucking bullshit is what they are." Elora picked the cigarette pack up, and threw it. She had a good throwing arm. It went far across the road and slammed into the parkade wall. "You know I am a cancer survivor, Enid. Breast cancer didn't kill me. Fuck that. Cancer won't get us. I don't want to see any more cigarettes."

The cigarettes were quickly destroyed by the pouring rain, so there was no sense in Enid trying to retrieve them, even if she wanted to.

Despite the rain, Enid and Elora were in no hurry to say goodbye, so they didn't care whether they got wet. After several minutes, they hugged each other tightly, and Elora got back into the Miata.

"Thank you!" Enid said, feeling lighter without the cigarettes, but not sure at all she wouldn't buy a new pack when she landed.

"No problema, lady," said Elora, laying rubber as she peeled out. "Get laid!" she shouted out the window as she pulled away.

Enid laughed and stepped into the empty airport. There were no lineups. She was very rapidly on the plane, masked, in a socially distanced seat, stretching out along her own entire row. She felt herself grieving the absence of her children, who were healthy and wonderful but whom she no longer saw half of the time. Even if they were right next to her, they had grown too big for her to say to them, "Look, we are flying in the sky—in the sky!" and to have their excitement spill out all around her as they peered out the windows. Enid exhaled and let herself miss their tiny faces and chubby hands and the past.

It was new for Enid to let herself miss the past. She had spent many years running away from her past, but now she wanted to grieve the identity and the love and the life she thought she had, and did not—grieve the fact that she would never be Arthur's widow, never be allowed, really, to grieve him openly. She resolved to let it wash over her so that when she returned she would be able to embrace her children in the present, to embrace the present, to embrace herself in the present, this new identity as a divorced woman, ready. Ready for new affairs, new loves, new sex, new adventures.

As the plane lurched eastward over the Atlantic, Enid was taken back to a memory of the view out of the dirty windows of the Greyhound bus she had taken the opposite way all of those years ago— leaving Calgary to go to law school in Kingston. This trip was trans-Atlantic. Air travel was necessary, but part of Enid wanted to feel the distance and to ride the ocean waves in a ship much as she had seen the prairies and then the woods roll by. She wanted to experience the ocean crossing as she had experienced the five-day journey overland across Canada—to take in the terrain change, to see Canada and feel the emotionality of its massiveness. Enid wanted to re-experience that turbulent and necessary journey, now departing for places she had never been, but she wanted a homecoming, to understand the difference in the space, not to erase the past, not to rewind the tape on her marriage but to somehow make sense of it, not gloss it over. She contented herself with closing her eyes and remembering the way the thunderclouds had looked over Saskatchewan wheat fields, rolling and flashing in the summer sky. This journey was in a way a wake for her married life, the life she had felt conflicted about anyway, the life that never felt quite hers, that never felt quite true, but that was her borrowed shell for so many years, her shelter. So unreal even now as to be almost a dream. But the kids are real, she reminded herself: her loves.

The Gateway

When the Air Canada plane descended from the blue sky, finding land among the blue waters of the Aegean, and landed in Athens, Enid was jolted out of a memory of their elderly marital therapist saying to her: "Enid, he doesn't care what you want." He had repeated it. "He does not care what you want." She shuffled into the bustling airport with the other passengers, into the long line for COVID tests.

Her nose stinging and head aching from the swab, Enid took a small plane to Naxos, one of many Greek Islands in the Aegean Sea. In fact it is the largest of the Cyclades islands, sitting in the heart of the Aegean Sea. White buildings, tawny yellow grass, Mediterranean blue sea, and the long, sandy expanse of Plaka Beach had appeared out the airplane window as she landed. Enid had come here for these things and also because the number of COVID cases in the Greek Islands at that time in the fall of 2020 was incredibly low: They had reported three. Mostly, though, Enid had come for the archaeological sites that Naxos offers, owing to her love of classical mythology. She had come to explore the ruins. Naxos has a temple to Demeter inland from its coast. And the most iconic of the archaeological sites of Naxos is Portara—the giant, brown, rectan-gular gate of an unfinished ancient temple dedicated to the Greek god Apollo.

Enid planned her trip to Naxos to see the Temple of Demeter and also what the island is best known for: an unfinished ruin. Its landmark is a gate, a massive marble gate to a temple dedicated to Apollo that was never finished. This towers over the seafront in the Chora, or central market, which were easily visible from the restaurants in the harbour. So how appropriate, thought Enid, that Naxos was the gateway between her marriage and everything after, the beginning of her journey into the next chapters of her life. She had come here because the temple of Apollo at Naxos—Portara to be more precise—was only a gateway built in 530 BC, which had never been completed. It was, in myth, where Theseus, the hero of Athens, somewhat like a Hellenic King Arthur, had abandoned Ariadne, and she had been rescued there, or abducted, depending upon the story, and Dionysus, the god of wine and debauchery, had abducted her. This was where Dionysian festivities had been held.

It was strange for Enid, all of this heat and blue sky and solitude, even the windswept, outdoor casual interactions, people nearly always devoid of masks. No one asked her questions. There were no children to fuss over, and no husband to tend to or fight with. Despite Elora, she did buy cigarettes and smoked them on the open deck of her room at the boutique hotel she stayed at, a small white structure. She could see the ocean from it. By day, she explored the ruins and the beaches, renting a four-wheel scooter. (They wouldn't let a Canadian have a two wheeler because, apparently, North Americans can't really drive.) By night, she walked the winding laneways in Naxos Chora, the main town of Naxos, taking in its mixture of Venetian and Cycladic architecture. Above the Cycladic white-washed houses of Chora stood its imposing Venetian castle. She took pictures and texted them home to her kids. Stray cats all over Naxos reminded Enid of her own cat, Artemis, back home, plump and dejected in her declawed inability to hunt. But these were different—hungry but also wild, immersed in the intrigues of their complicated, feral lives, and waiting for scraps thrown by tourists. Enid gave the stray cats some calamari, and they ate it slowly and not right away. One large black-and-white tomcat watched Enid vigilantly, and then after she looked away, it was gone. Once he was fed, five other cats gathered around Enid as she ate her dinner. One cat in particular reminded her of the cat, Spanx, she had as a child and teen—Enid's long-lost cat, the one that had disappeared while she was in hospital recovering from the accident.

On the second night, the whole ruins then took an interesting spin: a Greek man in a café offered to buy Enid a drink, and she sized him up. He was nice enough and somewhat handsome, and he asked if he knew her; he said he remembered her face. Was that a line? Likely. Of course it was. It was one that worked. He offered to show Enid around the Temple of Apollo in the dark, stepping deftly along the cobblestones, clearly knowing the way.

And how appropriate that it was there, on a cool rock, in the darkness beside this gate, that Enid let the Greek man, Constantin, whom she had met only minutes before in a café, like a stray cat, quietly corner her and, rapidly, have his way. She wanted that too. To know it was possible. To know she could still be with a man. To have the last touch she had felt not be Arthur's. The closure. She walked away from him with a light wave, and on her way back to her hotel, she saw cats that reminded her of the man in the cafe—the same look on their faces: patient, calm, waiting.

The Greek climate, thought Enid, as she travelled the dusty, winding roads on her scooter, is perfectly situated as a foundation for the cradle of civilization, which it is of course because it will yield fruit if effort is expended. The Mediterranean climate, Enid figured, encourages and fosters effort and requires effort but will satisfactorily produce if you work for it. On the whole, the travels were... satisfying. The classic ruins were magnificent, and the medieval ruins had their own beauty. She loved looking at the white church, with its round roof, overlooking the sea. The white buildings had a pure, satisfying smoothness, and the ground was dry. Enid went to the temple for Demeter. It was on a dry hill overlooking the Aegean sea, away from the fishing villages and the bustle of the marketplace, Demeter, goddess of fertility and grain, had a shrine that still stood.

Perhaps, thought Enid, that's the necessary foundation of civilization or democracy anyway: the notion that you can succeed if you try, a geography and a climate that make it possible. Fertile soil, but soil requiring effort. Some places are so forbidding that effort is discouraged because it feels pointless, and other places are so welcoming that, again, effort is discouraged, but the Greek islands seemed to hit a sweet spot in terms of climate: It will yield fruit and grain, but only if you work for it.

Constantin said there was a great energy in the spot where he kissed her, laid her down, and, rapidly, though with her clear consent, made love to her.

That night Enid facetimed Elora, gasping, she said, "It was like a re-enactment, an enactment of a Dionysian ritual. I had a spiritual experience."

Elora laughed and laughed, so hard that the image of her face shook. "Sure baby. That's what he'd love you to think. Whatever, honey, that's what you want to think too. But get real. That was just a local fucking a tourist. And I'm sure it was a completely unique and special moment. No doubt this was the very first time he did the exact same thing. I'm sure it was completely spontaneous too. Props to you both for getting your needs met, Enid, but give me a fucking break."

Enid was still breathless. "It's like I have gone from reading myths to suddenly living one!"

"Woah, I'm glad you got laid. Well done. But chill my friend! You are over-driving your headlights. This is not your next husband. I mean, God forbid. That's basically how you got together with the poor man's King Arthur, the tiny prick in the first place. Little Enid arrives in a new place and finds security. First guy that smiles at her is Prince Charming. Never mind that she's never seriously talked to anyone else. Nope. Nope. Fucking Nope."

"I know. I remembered what you said. Men are not the plot. I walked away from him with the words 'nice to meet you' and did not look back."

"Fuck ya! And there's another on the next island."

"No. I think that's it for this vacation. Going to focus on relaxing and seeing the sights."

"That, is also a good idea. If you read true crime, it's probably a safer strategy."

"What? You're the one who told me to get laid!"

"Yeah, but not with a local, Enid. Are you fucking crazy?"

"I feel like there's something problematic about this approach you are recommending. Something about orientalism or xenophobia or something." Enid chuckled, a low laugh that reminded her of her father's.

"I don't give a fuck if it's problematic or classist or some shit. Just stay alive."

"That is the plan."

They hung up.

And, Enid thought, as she fell asleep, the local and Elora were both fooled if they thought he was the only participant in the exchange whose motives were cynical. Enid's actions had perhaps not been that kind. He had a sadness about him, like that stray tomcat. Enid, like Artemis, she thought, was meant to be a hunter too, on her own journey, her own adventure, and she would not be waylaid there unduly at this ruined gate. Maybe, Enid thought as her flight took off the next day, it was best to think of it as a moment of connection, with humanity, with Greece, a moment that settled the question of whether she was desirable, whether she would ever have sex again, almost frighteningly quickly. Enid left Naxos having seen, and learned, in the ruins, that she remained an attractive woman and that there would be other men. She left resolved that the project of her journey was not to find the next one. She was on the hunt for something else: to find a satisfying life for herself, a life she could be proud of, that her kids could respect.

Atlantis

The small propeller plane lurched into the clear blue Aegean sky and took Enid to Santorini. Or, more properly, to the island chain of Thira, volcanic islands sitting in the Aegean Sea, halfway between Athens and Crete. Santorini is actually the island of Thera, which is actually Atlantis, the city that sank into the sea two thousand years ago. The island chain is a ring around a volcano, and now only the tops of the cliffs survive. So, Santorini, in a sense, is an occupation on top of ruins, where the ruins are submerged under the sea. It's incredibly beautiful, a shocking testament to resilience.

Thira is itself a ruin. It was once circular and known as Strongili (the Round One). Before Classical Greece emerged, a huge volcanic eruption caused the centre of Strongili to sink, leaving a caldera with jagged, towering cliffs along its east side. It was also, they say, what they called Atlantis. Enid stepped off the plane and onto the hot tarmac into the world she had read about in myth as long as she could remember. She tore off her mask once outside, inhaled and exhaled, breathing in the dry, Mediterranean air with a mix of joy and disbelief.

Enid was sitting in the egg-shaped infinity pool in her magnificent hotel overlooking the city of Fira, high on the cliff tops of Santorini, Greece. It was literally breathtaking. Hauling her suitcase from the taxi, Enid had begun to regret those Naxos cigarettes. When she and the porter arrived at the door of her hotel, her breath was taken away for another reason. The soft white building looked down the sharp cliffs onto the sea. Pumice stone, soft and white, was the island's traditional building material. The buildings, perched atop cliffs, looked like coral reefs, or like teeth by day. By night, they looked like heaven. It was almost unbelievably beautiful. The volcano caldera around which the islands of Thira gather is called Nea Kameni—new birth. This is, they say, the volcano that sank Atlantis and, more recently, killed a town in 1956. The volcano is mother and destroyer, the ash from which the fertile volcanic soil of Santorini is ever made anew. So it is not just a place of ruins but also of rebirth, a place of a relationship between the two that Enid wanted to understand. She took a tourist boat to the centre of the island chain and hiked, breathlessly, up the side of the caldera, along the gray scrabbly rock to where the centre of the active volcano could be seen, steaming. Then she and the other tourists on the journey were taken to a narrow bay where the salt water was muddy and warm, and they bathed in the hot springs from the volcano.

When Enid was married, except for three occasions when she was enraged, she never took her wedding ring off. She had developed a callous on that finger. They had cut the ring off at the jewelers, slicing through it with flecks of gold dust flying around her finger. And, now, the callous was still there, and even as she was sitting there, in Greece, she felt the callous and sometimes thought the ring was still there, like they say amputees feel their missing limbs.

Octopus enhances libido, said a short, dark-haired waiter at the cafe, who tells Enid he is in love with her now, after he asked where her husband was.

Enid shrugged, saying "no husband anymore." She looked up at him quizzically to see if he was serious. He seemed to mean it, at least in the limited way a man might mean it for an off night. He looked older than her but probably was not. He smiled and said to come back later, and he would show her how much he loved her. Enid paid her bill rapidly and did not go back. She was finished with that aspect of her journey, at least on this trip. She was hunting but not for a man. Still, while in Greece, Enid ate octopus every day.

When Enid started clearing away the rubble of the ruined narrative arc of her marriage, she remembered, and started to feel again, the heart-pounding nervousness of her teen years. She remembered, by the Aegean Sea, beneath the narrative she had carefully crafted of her marriage, what she had never felt about Arthur, that she had never craved and hungered for him in that passionate way—that their chemistry had been pleasant but not electric, that the creeping, lurking suspicion that their perfect love storyline was not quite accurate, not quite true, had its roots there. It was like the fourteen-year-old self long hidden inside her prim, suburban shell, was stretching. She wasn't like the hermit crab looking for another shell to protect her though.

After going back to her hotel to change into her swimsuit, Enid went down to the sea and sat down on a large gray rock. After calling her children, Enid facetimed her friends Elora and Kat in a group chat, eager to hear the news of how COVID-19 was in Ottawa, eager to find out whether her friends were safe.

"I saw Arthur with some really, really young woman. I was walking around with little Jimmy after his nap this afternoon. And there he was: Arthur the idiot in his Tesla," said Kat, Enid's long-time friend from law school, a tall, soft-spoken blonde woman who ran marathons and worked as a corporate lawyer. "Thought you should know."

"Oh Jesus jumping Jesus," Elora said, "Midlife crisis Ken hopped into a sports car with an offensively young woman. Your idiot ex-husband has such bad writers."

"You need," said Kat, "someone who can write his own lines." She paused and disappeared from view as the sound of a child crying filled the background. There was a rustling sound and she re-emerged with a tow-headed toddler.

"Jimbo Jim!" Enid said merrily, "little man!"

The toddler giggled, his blue eyes glinting adorably. Kat smiled wanly and hugged him, and the fatigue was evident in her eyes from across the Atlantic.

"COVID-19 lockdown must be something else with your fella there, Kat,"

"Yeah, it's a heckuva thing," said Kat, "no childcare, no nanny, and Tom's in an essential field as a paramedic. So here I am writing affidavits with my assistant here, Mr. Jim."

"I'm so sorry, Kat. What a nightmare."

Kat smiled wanly, again, "Worse things," she said, "happen at sea." She went on. "But I gotta say, Enid, I don't feel sorry for you. Yes, Arthur ripped your heart out. Yes, that's shit. But you are off on your rich white lady existential journey, your *Eat, Pray, Love* shit and that's a privilege. People are dying."

"I agree with you, Kat. Times are tough."

Elora sniffed and returned to the earlier subject. "I do not assume," said Elora, "that she needs anyone at all."

"Everybody needs somebody sometimes," said Kat, "everybody falls in love somehowwwww..."

"Everybody finds somebody someday... there's no telling where love may appear. Gotta love some Dean Martin." Enid laughed and agreed. "Arthur does have bad writers. But the frustrating part is that Arthur made me a cliché too. He could write his own life with a lame, tired, and trite plotline, but the fact he had pulled me into that, leaving me a bored, bourgeois wifey, was incredibly frustrating." As she had often felt the past few years, Enid, sardonically, told Elora and Kat she felt she had been miscast.

"Meh," said Elora, "he's not the director. Quit the role. Move. You're not a tree. Kat, how would Jimbo Jim there feel about a visit with his Aunt El, so you could have a nap?"

"An inspired suggestion, my friend," said Kat. "Tomorrow would work."

They hung up, and Enid put her phone down on the rock, and dove down towards the lost kingdom of Atlantis, somewhere below here, into the blue, blue Aegean Sea.

Camelot

The COVID-19 pandemic was a tragedy for millions who became ill and others who died. It was devastating for the global economy and, in short, a dramatic blow to all of humanity. It was not just Enid's nail art that felt the impact of this. COVID-19 meant Enid faced significant risks when travelling as well as moral questions and stigma for doing it, and she was also supposed to quarantine upon return from international travel. Just as Enid had not been good at being grounded when a teen, and had been terrible at bed rest when ill during pregnancy, she did not do well with her quarantine. She did not have COVID-19, and she knew it, having received a negative test before leaving Greece. She tried to get another one on arrival to Ottawa, but the healthcare providers wouldn't even let her get the test, since she showed no symptoms. So, she was supposed to quarantine in her home, the home that Arthur was occupying to insist upon his claim to it, for fourteen days. This did not go well. Enid escaped periodically, to ride her e-scooter down the road, go for a walk, or even get a coffee. And, unfortunately for her, the police checked in. An officer by the name of Constable Adora kept calling and stopping by. Even two weeks after the end of her quarantine period, he called to say they should meet. He'd read her Twitter feed. He'd read her Facebook.

She called her old friend James Hughes, who was a criminal defence lawyer. James was the one who had, many years ago, defended her teenage boyfriend Bruno when she was the designated prosecutor in the matter, back in Ottawa before she fled to Cincinnati under the cover of Arthur's work. They had stayed in touch casually when she went to Cincinnati. She had never told him why she left the criminal law back then. It occurred to her that this omission would seem likely quite irrelevant today. Time had moved on. Enid simply called James to ask whether she should respectfully decline the opportunity for a meeting with this officer. James agreed. "Are the cops not busy? It sort of seems like they aren't busy," Enid said. James chuckled. "They're not. Very little crime during COVID-19." So Enid was basically being harassed by the police, or at least by this particular officer, after Arthur and his family had reported her to the police for having gone for a walk.

Enid did not have COVID-19. She therefore did not give anyone COVID-19. And despite his intriguing name, she did not have to meet with the officer. No fines were paid. The quarantine period ended, and her civil liberties were returned. When the quarantine ended, she could again go outside, at least to the extent permissible in the lockdowns that followed.

There was sadness and blankness in this silence, but there was also something else.

A feeling was beginning to stir. Enid had planned to tour the ruins, but she was beginning to notice something a bit surprising about herself that resonated with the ruins. She was not made of dust, like the dead of Pompeii, not crumbling. She was not made of rocks. She was alive underneath. And, when the ruins were blown away by the winds of change and divorce and aging, she felt herself growing stronger. She remembered what it was like to have a crush on someone, what it felt like to rely upon herself and her friends, and what it felt like to make her own choices. Enid felt a new spark of connection with the girl she had been, red haired and plump, running on prairie grass and laughing into the wind. She had truly come out of her shell.

In the midst of this, she'd bought a house, a red brick house by the canal in Ottawa, for herself and the kids. A downtown home, in the midst of cafés, from which she could walk to work. She was no longer encased in a suburban shell, no longer obligated to play the same role of housewife, doctor's wife. This was not to say she did not play a role. Enid was now a divorced woman, the source of some scandal, about her travel, and her poor performance at quarantine, and also, about the men she was now sleeping with. She kept this from her children, but she did not hide from Arthur that there were evenings she went out. Enid unabashedly decided to simply enjoy her life, to show her children what empowerment and emancipation might look like, for their sake as well as hers—and to show her children that she was alive underneath.

This year was a ruin of Enid's grand plans too: COVID-19 had interrupted the middle of her *Eat, Pray, Love* midlife indulgence, so she was sitting by a campfire in her backyard with Elora instead of on a Dominican beach.

It reminded Enid of earthquakes, of people trapped beneath rubble, or of those Chilean miners that had been rescued, after days underground, tapping. She was starting to feel a tapping. That's how she felt sometimes. And, other times, there were bad nights. Like that windy fall night when she called Arthur's cell phone four times at midnight, as she walked along the canal in the November darkness. There was just so much history between them. She wondered, then, in the darkness, looking up at the stars, whether something was salvageable. Every night for twenty-five years, she'd wished on a star that she and Arthur would love each other forever. It seemed strange and impossible to abandon that, as she walked through the gusts and darkness. But, he didn't answer, which was probably for the best. By the time morning rolled around, she had composed herself. There was no way around the aching she felt in the darkness, and the only way around it was through it. Enid, after all, had always loved myths.

When her mother Judith tried to tell her Santa wasn't real, Enid had rejected the assertion, saying Judith was wrong, insisting a cabal of older men met at shopping malls and distributed the toy-giving duties between themselves. At age ten, Enid was a holdout. She wanted to believe in magic. She had wanted to believe in Arthur, and in their marriage, too, despite that nagging itch, that whisper just about below audibility, these past few years and even before, that something wasn't right. And, anyway, Arthur didn't answer. His phone just went to voicemail, or more precisely to a generic message saying his voice mail was full.

It reminded her of a few of his choice statements to her as they were separating, the morning the moving truck had come that September. Enid had, in the last moment, looked back at him standing on the porch and ran to him, humiliatingly, begging him not to separate. She had said, "But I love you. If we were both drowning, I would save you. I would choose you. That's what love is."

Arthur had replied softly, "I would also choose me."

Enid had said to him, "I don't believe it. You are kind and hiding it; you have a lot of good qualities. Maybe we were right for each other at the time, but not now."

"Believe it." Arthur scoffed. "You had merits too. You were fertile." He walked away.

Enid figured she had better start believing it, believing that her vision of Arthur had been an illusion, that she had followed him unwisely. So, she'd bought a house close to where she and Arthur had lived many years before, when she felt powerful, when she had practiced law, before they moved to the US, before they had kids. Not to recapture her past but to find herself in the present.

Even so, even with all of this ugly truth about Arthur emerging, Enid still remembered that, once upon a time, there had been a perfect summer afternoon. In fact there had been many. There were videos of it that Enid had—of her and Arthur playing with their children in the swimming pool, flipping them around and dancing. At least they had had those. They had those perfect summer afternoons. Many years of them. More. There were six years of summer afternoons at their house in Ottawa, six years of Christmas parties, and morning gifts from Santa too. Many years of children jumping into leaves. Before that, years in Cincinnati too. Those years now felt like a distant dream, another life, and perhaps the good news was that Enid felt like she had stepped back into her own life.

With Arthur, she had confused form with content: he knew the forms she had been taught—the right words, the right lexicon. She had mistaken his classical education for a love of the things she loved. He knew classical mythology, but he didn't love it. He did not think the way she did. He did not think in metaphors. Really, he hardly thought of other people at all.

That fall was hard on the children. Teens, locked down in the pandemic, their lives in disarray. They were a captive audience to their parents' divorce. They smoked weed. They gave each other ear piercings too and told Enid to go fuck herself more than once. Freya had her first kiss, when she also puked and peed her pants. Milestones were passing in the midst of all of it.

Morgana said to Enid at the breakfast table. "You are my second favourite parent."

Enid cried.

They were a long distance in time from that perfect afternoon when her kids were young. They were also far from where Enid had wanted to be as a parent, from where she had vowed to be, thinking of her loss of her own mother's companionship and mentorship when Judith had been put into in-patient psychiatric care when Enid was in her teens. Enid had wanted so desperately to have a trouble-free experience of parenting, to give her kids a solid foundation, and it was not possible, in the end, despite all appearances to the contrary, and the tiny home, and the carefully landscaped garden in the ideal neighbourhood with the children's surgeon father. Good on paper was not necessarily good after all.

"Ibn Khaldun," Enid said to Morgana, "was this medieval Islamic writer who noticed that, when the nomads came in from the desert to conquer a city, they would invariably lay siege to the city, leave it in ruins, and then, over time, rebuild it the same way. How does one rebuild differently? I wanted to build you a perfect world, Morgana. I wanted you to have a perfect life."

Morgana said, "Then you were arrogant, Mom. You thought you were better than everyone else."

Morgana, thought Enid, was harsh and incisive, and she was right. How could Enid not simply have the same relationship, the same feeling of being in the wrong shell, over and over again? How could she be with her children, even be with a partner, and be present, fully present, and have him be present too? Was that an illusion? Was happiness possible? Could Guinevere's story arc have another alternative ending, after all? Could Guinevere have built a golden age of peace and prosperity on her own, without Arthur? And what might such a utopian capital, built from Guinevere's ambitions and work, have looked like? How could Enid begin to envision a feminist Camelot?

December

Christmas decorations and lights appeared on many houses. The winter holidays approached in the midst of COVID-19. Lockdowns grew, and infection rates surged while the promise of a vaccine emerged and the first doses arrived. The first vaccine was administered in the UK on the day that Arthur's father was buried, having died of the disease.

Arthur's father died in England in December 2020, almost a year into the pandemic and, ironically, well into the vaccine effort. He'd become infected that November and spent weeks in the intensive care unit with COVID-19 pneumonia, without visitors, before passing on at last. Arthur didn't tell Enid about the illness until the death. Arthur had been raised by a series of nannies and then in boarding schools while his parents travelled for diplomatic posts on behalf of the UK government. His parents had since retired, and Arthur visited them seldom. Their children had seen their paternal grandparents three times in seventeen years. Arthur never complained about his parents, and birthday and Christmas cards were dutifully exchanged, but there was rarely shared laughter, and there were few reminiscences.

"How are you, Arthur?" Enid asked him when she went to pick up their kids at the access transfer.

"Well, you know. Life goes on. He was old," said Arthur, lightly.

"But life does not go on. He died. Arthur, I am so sorry that he died."

Arthur shrugged, but his eyes betrayed him, as they had so often that fall, and he looked away.

The funeral was not in person, but via Zoom. This made it less awkward for her, so Enid attended, using her iPhone in her car. She noticed Arthur did not log in. He was busy, as always, at work.

A friend of the family who Enid didn't know delivered the eulogy, "He liked what he liked," said the elderly man, wiping his nose. "And you could be sure of him." Arthur's mother, visible on screen, started to cry.

Enid realized that was what it had been: She had not been sure of Arthur. He had shifted, depending on the moment, depending upon the audience, and he had always been performing for the audience. She wanted the unperformed, the certainty of someone's idiosyncrasies, someone who was who they were, unapologetically. She wanted to reach out and feel a warm hand, a distinct hand with its grooves and hair and imperfections, pressing hers back.

As snow was falling, Enid sat in on the Zoom call watching the small memorial service while waiting outside her lawyer's office to sign the separation agreement. Due to COVID-19, she had to wait in her parked car. The parking lot faced a funeral home where someone else's life was being celebrated. Black limousines pulled slowly away from the building, just as the concluding music swelled out of the speakers on Enid's iPhone. She started sobbing because this was still another loss in her life, even if she hadn't known Arthur's father well. She opened her window to feel the cold, fresh air on her hot cheeks. Her tears felt cold on her face. The wind whipped at her hair, and it seemed like mortality struck her physically in the face with its cold blast in that moment, and she wondered if she would ever again hold another hand in hers.

Melt

New life blossoms in the ruins.
—Friedrich Schiller

"Do any of us know how to rebuild?" typed Enid into her Facebook status on her browser window. She deleted it and did not post. Enid wondered maybe if it was a peculiar consequence, an echo of her prairie childhood, to not have a way to understand how we can rebuild over ruins. So many people lived over layers and layers of evidence of human occupation. Rome is built atop Rome atop Rome after all, the contemporary streets above the medieval ones, above the ancient city. But Calgary is built on the open prairie, where the Indigenous people lived so harmoniously with the grasses and skies that they left almost no trace. Enid had not been able to glide through life without leaving behind a wreck. She wanted to go around the world, after seeing in Santorini, the cities built on the ruins of Atlantis. She wanted to go to Peru, to Spain, to Nepal, to see new life built around ruins, new life built quickly around the wreck of the old, most importantly, to be rebuilt somehow differently, to not just replicate past patterns but to choose a new way of living, a new beginning that would make sense around the ruins of hopes and dreams and aspirations.

The future? She typed that question into the status bar too, then deleted that text as well, and closed her laptop with a snap. What future was there to plan for in the midst of this listlessness?

Time would tell. Her social media profiles had stopped to a large extent, and her blogs had grown silent. This was true of a lot of people, mind you, in the pandemic, when it became distasteful to be announcing news with #Blessed captioning in with people dying and others isolating all around you. Yet for Enid, it was more personal. After a difficult adolescence and after always feeling like a fish out of water at Queen's Law School among the children of the privileged, and with her marriage to Arthur, a ticket into their world but hollow in the middle, she had posted on social media almost vengefully, looking not just for affirmation but to incite envy, and now, that is not how she wanted to walk in the world. She now felt comfortable not looking for that shell to protect her.

Enid smiled to herself; good things were afoot. Precisely what were they? She was not telling. She was secretly travelling during the pandemic lockdowns, quietly pushing boundaries, and it made her feel free. Now, Enid thought as she roamed the empty halls of her law firm's office, it was not just her sitting in a house watching the cars go by, itching for participation and purpose in a wider world. Now, to quote the COVID-19 cliché, "We were in this together." Everyone was trapped in the pandemic world. Enid had always felt alone, like the Okotoks Rock smacked down in the prairie far from the mountain chains, but the loss of her marriage and the pandemic isolation were leading her into new friendships. In the midst of quarantine. Enid began to feel that she was part of a community.

Then, as she learned from Sybil, who let it out casually at dinner, Arthur was dating a twenty-year-old medical receptionist who used to babysit the kids. Enid sighed. Arthur was a cliché through and through. She resolved to say nothing about it, but when she picked up the kids that week, she said to him, "Sooner or later, Arthur, whether she works for you or not," Enid said, "your twelve-year-old girlfriend is going to have an opinion. It will happen." And then, she drove off, spinning her wheels on the gravel of his driveway, wishing a big cloud of dust would emerge and cover him as she drove away. It did not.

As Enid drank her wine that night she thought: COVID-19—fuck. It was like a broken lifeboat. Enid's plan to recover, escape, run away from her marriage, her latter day *Eat, Pray, Love* middle-class midlife reframing, was getting jettisoned by the global pandemic. Now, instead of wallowing indulgently in self-centred lament, sitting on a beach in the Dominican contemplating her next steps, she was holed up in her new home in a January lockdown with five teenage children being homeschooled while her son's ability to stay in bed playing on his computer began to make her worry if he would get bedsores and the older girls sneaked out with their in-withdrawal-from-hockey boyfriends.

This was not Enid's planned self-actualization journey. Her plan had not involved shepherding her teens through Romeo-and-Juliet style balcony escapes and relationship dramas just at the time hers had fallen apart. Every time they made a plan—to holiday, to go to summer camp, or to work at their parttime jobs—it had to be rescheduled and replanned numerous times.

Enid was concerned. She had been incredibly fertile as a young woman, unknowingly pregnant when she miscarried in a car crash as a teen, and then pregnant almost continuously when she was first married to Arthur. Thankfully, her first baby had been born in good health, and she was blessed with Freya. Enid did not resent this fecundity. She had loved motherhood. So much so, that she was almost continuously pregnant for six years. Her babies were born in quick succession. Freya and Morgana came together, and the two were inseparable as childhood frenemies. Then petite, big-eyed, and gentle Sybil was born, bringing her curious heart and love of water, followed by the little warrior, Wolfgang. Last but not least came the lovely Lenore. They had been these perfect, golden children, that shone and glistened on Enid's Instagram and ruled her heart, and now they were unruly teens, becoming their own people. They were as fierce as Enid had been as a child and teen and were smooth and precise like their father. They told her they did not consent to photo sharing and that what her teenage kids disparagingly called her "Karening on the socials" had to stop. They were sharp tongued, all of them, witty as hell, and lively. They were the best parts of Arthur and of Enid. And they were a hell of a handful.

Enid's divorce plan was not going to plan at all. There were the COVID-19 masks everywhere, whirling across downtown streets like tumbleweed in a spaghetti western, and social judgments abounded on the social media platforms where she had once been living, laughing and loving and frequently posting the hashtag #Blessed.

In April 2021, as spring blossomed in Nepal so did a COVID-19 outbreak at Everest base camp. Instead of trekking to Everest, Enid found herself huddled over a backyard campfire with her friend Elora, laughing in the goddamn minus-twenty cold, eating red Thai curry because they weren't allowed to socialize indoors in light of a strict lockdown. It must have felt like this to live through a war. Later, in her mess of renovations, with the laundry machines unplugged and a gaping hole in the basement left overnight by contractors, Enid was doing an online dance class suggested by Elora on Zoom in her living room while the kids visited Arthur. But in the face of all of this, Enid realized that she was happy. She was happy in her living room all alone just because she liked the new light fixture. She was happy sipping wine on the porch with her friends. She was made happy by small things.

Half the time now, Enid was not responsible for the day-to-day care of her kids. This was so weird. She had more free time every second week than she'd had in years. She enjoyed it. She missed her children, missed their loud, happy chaos, but she also loved listening to instrumental music, lighting scented candles, and relishing stillness. She had been hungry for stillness, for travel, and for a return to herself. Enid came across a picture of herself at fourteen, taken in the autumn when her skin was glowing from the summer sun, and she was smiling so widely in it, and this was taken before her life was shattered by so many things: the car accident, her mother's breakdown, the moves, childbirth, her divorce. But she recognized herself in it now.

It was hard to think that her golden children, for whom she had so carefully tried to curate a perfect world, had now suffered the breakdown of their parents' marriage. That was just hard.

March

It was March again now, a full year into the pandemic, and Enid was slipping and sliding over the mushy and icy ruins of winter on Ottawa streets near the melting canal. Mud caked over the ice. It was no longer pristine. It was dark and slippery, littered with dark puddles of uncertain depth. The morning was warm but smelled of rotting things, like a hangover from winter. This seemingly endless pandemic felt like a hangover from life.

She had been separated for six months now. Enid had her own home, albeit one under construction, her own car, her own new furniture, and she had routines that structured her days. COVID-19 raged on, and 2.1 million people had died, and her entire life had unravelled, and she was weaving the threads of herself and her family back together. Or trying. It was not easy to feel like anything was progressing in this lockdown mess.

Evidently, they had reached the no-one-gives-a-shit phase of the pandemic in Zoom meetings, which was clear from the fact that Enid's colleague Tilly lit up a cigarette in a department meeting that Monday morning, and her other colleague, Miranda, started breastfeeding with no blanket and the camera on. Today's meetings were a far cry from the smooth, suited events that had taken place in gleaming boardrooms high in the sky pre-COVID-19. Authenticity was more readily available, but the glamour was gone. Enid missed the glamour. She had, after all, been drawn back to law at least partly for the Louboutin shoes and the expensive heels with red soles that had been emblematic of freedom and glamour to a younger Enid.

Elora texted Enid: "Kill me."

Enid nodded absently at her computer screen while she texted her back, "Why? It's Friday, and the sun is shining"

"The sun never shines in Zoom court," replied Elora.

Enid smiled and resumed her inactivity, camera off, in a Microsoft teams meeting while she was doom scrolling through her social media profiles and the now old posts about *Tiger King*, sourdough bread, fun pandemic projects involving knitting and putting rainbows on windows, as well as banging pots and pans to show appreciation for frontline workers, reports of dolphins in Venetian canals, and tongue-in-cheek satirical replies about orcas in the Rideau Canal next to the Parliament buildings.

If she couldn't travel, she could surf the web. Enid opened up Google and looked up surfing in Canada, scrolling through pictures of Long Beach near Tofino. She moved on to pictures of the old growth forests at Clayoquot sound, in her suburban idyll, in cyberspace, she desperately craved a western sense of place, a sense of land, land where she belonged, and it was painful because, as the child of settlers, she knew she didn't really belong anywhere. There was no home country to hearken back to, and she also had no Indigenous claim to the land, to the prairies she had walked barefoot as a child. Enid was a wanderer, in cyberspace or elsewhere, and she had wanted so desperately to have not just any home but the perfect home. She had married Arthur in an attempt to secure that.

Air travel between provinces was discouraged during the pandemic, but Enid desperately wanted to return to Western Canada, to Calgary, for the first time in years, and she fantasized that time was not entirely linear, and she might land in 1997 and take up her life where she had left it after leaving for Queen's, to her life before she took a Greyhound bus east to university, before Arthur, before she became a lawyer, before she became Enid Kimble.

Time flies, or at least is a fugitive. It escapes us: Tempus fugit, it is trite to say, but true. There are links between the present and the past. Enid googled the Okotoks rock. The rock, after all, is still running. All of the rocks are shifting in geological time on their tectonic plates. Google revealed that there is a subduction zone on the BC Pacific coast; there are ongoing earthquakes. The mountains themselves were created by the movement of rocks.

"The Okotoks rock is part of a larger family," Enid said out loud, to Artemis and to no one in particular. She heard Morgana call across from the living room in an angry reply: "Who are you trying to convince?"

In her online travels via Google, Enid stumbled across a tiny place called Lund, BC, up on its western Sunshine Coast, a place they called the end of the road, or its beginning, depending upon how you look at it. It was the final kilometre of Highway 101. Or the first. A place where photos showed stairs on which someone had written that it was the boundary between the road and Desolation Sound, a marine ecological preserve on the unceded land of the Klahoose First Nation, where mountainous islands covered in pine and cliffs and ancient petroglyphs rose up around still, calm bays up to two-thousand feet deep, of ancient, blue water. Enid imagined herself diving into those waters in that place where the road ends in desolation, or desolation ends with a road, or the two are looped together, diving into that space between ruin and rebuilding, and she exhaled slowly.

They say the Indigenous people conceptualize time as a circle. Enid wanted to ride across that circle back. Where though? Into herself? Certainly into a more innocent moment, where she was cared for and laughing, a moment where she was a child. And this of course was impossible. Nothing stays the same. She could not even secure that safety for her own children, at least one of whom glowered at her at all times. All of the rocky surface features, all geological events arise from invisible inner processes—endless shifting. It was comforting to think that perhaps they were part of a larger whole. Enid, always the A student, did not know how the story would end, but she hoped there was, somewhere, somehow, a correct answer.

"Google, the oracle, reveals..."—Enid said aloud to Artemis, but softly this time, to avoid an irate reply from Morgana, since Artemis, unlike her teenage children, would still listen to a story she spun, and lay curled up on a pillow in her study, her paws scarred but no longer bandaged—"... that any scientific papers say that the Indigenous stories are reasonable records, covering an unknowable amount of time, of earthquakes and tsunamis along the entire Cascadia Subduction Zone." Enid smiled a little. "Artemis, one story says that earthquakes are people dancing. On Vancouver Island, the Nuu-chah-nulth people tell tales of mountain dwarves who invited a person to dance around their drum. When this person accidentally kicked the drum over, he got 'earthquake foot.'" Enid patted Artemis on her smooth, black head, and Artemis purred. "Earthquake foot, like I had on the gas pedal in my car accident, and the steps of the mountain dwarf set off vast tremors." She continued. "Even if they aren't people dancing, the stories tell about how all of the rocks are running, not just the Okotoks Rock so far from its family, but all of the Rocky Mountains. Off Vancouver Island, the North American tectonic plate meets the Juan De Fuca tectonic plate, and the Explorer plate too, and the Indigenous stories relate about Tsunamis and earthquakes. The punchline, Artemis, is these are stories about which historical records have been recently discovered by scientists. The stories may not be entirely factual, but they aren't untrue."

Enid continued talking softly to Artemis, closing her laptop now, "Artemis, Aristotle, in the *Nicomachean Ethics*, said that the goodness of an upright citizen is relative to the city of which he is a citizen. Which is another way of saying that you can be as loyal as a fart if you are a privileged WASP man with all sorts of opportunities to be an asshole. Which is maybe why I didn't know who Arthur was until it was so late in the game, hopefully not too late. And he will see little judgment for it—if you live in a city where you can do no wrong because of your position of power. It doesn't make you a good man to be considered an upright citizen. Let's be real: JFK cheated too." Enid pulled Artemis onto her lap. "And I still love JFK." She googled "John Fitzgerald Kennedy Camelot" and sighed a bit, scrolling through the photos of a mid-twentieth-century American presidency, a handsome man assassinated in his prime.

Enid didn't exactly feel like forgiving Arthur, but she did feel like releasing him. She felt like diving into those salty waters of Desolation Sound and letting it all go. With the computer closed, Enid held Artemis and felt less alone.

Going Home

April 2021 began with a discouraging dump of snow. It all seemed endless. There was hope on the horizon, but the horizon seemed to move as Enid approached it. She was tired. Every plan she'd made, every attempt at escape, was being frustrated and shut down. All of her attempts to continue her journey through ruins were met with resistance. Her flight to BC was cancelled. AstraZeneca vaccines, reputed to be dangerous, were being made available for people her age, Gen X, but she was having trouble getting one—calling pharmacy after pharmacy and finding no appointments available.

On April 23, Enid received a surprising phone call from her father, Atticus Alger, a retired professional writer, with whom she'd had warm but infrequent contact. "I've got a tip for you, Enid. A COVID-19 tip." The fact that he had dug up information was unsurprising. Atticus used to drive around with a police scanner in his black Ford Mustang when she was growing up, back when he was a crime reporter always chasing the news.

"Dad, I want to survive this."

"Fair enough. Are you willing to do something problematic? I got a line on a solution for you, Enid, but you will have to get on a plane."

"Tell me. I have to survive. I have five kids and a lot of work to do."

"Well, I heard something from an old friend at the Cardston RCMP detachment. Remember Jim Halston? Anyways, he works near the Piegan-Carway border crossing. Word is that the Montana native tribe, the Black-feet, have excess supply. They are gifting vaccines to neighbours across the border and not just Indigenous people. They are calling it an 'act of reconciliation.' An interesting development— a historic government-to-government, nation-to-nation act of reconciliation. It's called the Medicine

Line Clinic. The Montana Blackfeet contacted Health Canada as well as provincial and state officials. They will vaccinate anyone. They will give anyone who shows up either their first or second dose of the Moderna or the Pfizer vaccine. I checked it out. It's a joint effort between a ton of people, including the Blackfeet Tribe, the Blackfoot Confederacy, Siksika Nation, Piikani Nation, Blood Tribe, US Customs, Canada Border Services, and health officials from state and provincial governments, and federal governments on both sides. A huge collaboration, Enid—quite exciting! They have supplies for approximately one thousand. The tribe will distribute the Pfizer and Moderna vaccines over the next four days at the Piegan port of entry."

"They will vaccinate you," Atticus continued. "You just have to get there. I checked all of this out on social platforms. It's verified. They will vaccinate you if you can get here in the next four days. Fly to Calgary, and we can drive there. I'm going to go and report on it for my podcast. Come with me, and we'll both get our shots."

"Damn. That's a helluva scoop, Dad! I think I just will."

So she decided to fly home to survive COVID-19. And maybe it would help her survive her divorce.

Enid called Arthur. "I have to be away for a few days. We need to switch dates with the kids."

"Travelling again during COVID-19, Enid?" said Arthur, and she could hear the characteristic sneer. "How typical of you to flout the law."

"Oh these aren't laws," scoffed Enid, jokingly, brushing off the superior tone in his voice. "Arthur, they're regulations."

Arthur sniffed primly, as usual, clearly self-satisfied. "I guess we feel differently about the rule of law."

Enid rolled her eyes. "Discretion in enforcement is part of the rule of law, asshat. The laws are made up by people to achieve goals. They're not absolutes, Arthur. They're not gravity." She paused. "Arthur."

"What now?" He sniffed again.

"You're just some guy. You're not that special. You are a self-satisfied, judgmental prick who is smug and abrasive. And you have no balls. Call 911 if you want to."

"Nah," said Arthur, "I'll switch the dates. And you can fly straight to hell. I might call the police; I might not. I want you to be surprised. It would be fun if you got caught and more fun if you don't see it coming."

The Medicine Line

On Wednesday, April 28, Enid flew to Calgary on an almost empty plane, masked, in the midst of the stay-at-home order imposed in Ontario. It was a bumpy ride, but breathtaking as the plane started its descent from its cruising altitude to the prairie city. The mountains were sharply visible in the distance, and the glittering skyline of Calgary's downtown core rose just outside her window. Enid was able to pick out Nose Hill Park in the distance, and even, with a sharp intake of breath, to see the white roof of her childhood home beside it. Enid felt, briefly, as though she really was doing what she had fantasized about doing, travelling back through the circle of time and landing in 1997.

Enid internally cheered as the wheels hit the tarmac. It had been a long time since she'd made a trip to Calgary, where she had grown up. She was going home for the first time in twenty years, without a celebratory agenda, not going as a hometown girl made good. She was going, to some extent, in failure, for shelter. She felt like that hermit crab again—looking for another shell to protect her. She was going to see her family and to greet them, not as a success story but as a woman whose marriage had failed. Enid also wanted to see the rock, the Okotoks Erratic, to see it in its field among the grasses, that spectacular ruin of the last ice age. Enid landed at the airport in Calgary at 4:00 p.m. Mountain time. She always liked the sound of that. As she walked through the almost empty halls of the arrivals area, it was painfully clear she had only, in fact, travelled back in time two hours. What few people were scattered among the halls were wearing masks. She was overtaken by a surge of emotion and a flashback of landing in Calgary with Arthur when they arrived for their wedding, nearly twenty-five years ago. Then, the arrivals area had been full of laughing family and friends. Enid's mother had been holding a sign that said, "Bride and Groom." There had been laughter and flowers. And now, Enid was arriving mid-pandemic and mid-divorce to an empty hallway, a janitor sweeping the floor, and silence.

On the ring road outside the shuttered airport, hollowed out by COVID -19, only a few passengers scuttled around hastily in masks. Atticus picked her up in the arrival lane at the Calgary airport. He was retired now and grey-haired, smaller than he had seemed in her childhood, and was sitting in a Cadillac Escalade, an updated vehicle to replace his classic Ford Mustang. He rolled down the tinted window and called gruffly to Enid with a mischievous grin. "Welcome to the wild west"

Atticus piloted his car smoothly down the Deerfoot Trail. They would have to drive two hours to get to the Piegan-Carway border crossing near Babb, Montana. The road to the border crossing took them south along the Deerfoot Trail through Calgary, past the skyscrapers of the downtown core, and then onto Highway 2 south. They took a detour and went past the Okotoks Rock, the place where many years ago Enid had crashed her boyfriend Bruno's car.

They stopped there and stepped outside into the cool spring evening, and Atticus had a cigarette. He no longer smoked in his car. Enid had never let him know she smoked. The suburbs had spread towards the rock now, with the urban sprawl facilitated by the open land of the prairie. Beige McMansions were visible on the horizon, what Enid called the large, hastily constructed, anonymous looking suburban homes that had cropped up on the urban sprawl of the prairie in boom years. Okotoks had grown, and there was an arena next to the rock. Enid felt dizzy when she first looked at the rock. It was the first time she had seen it since that Halloween night all those years ago, except for the many times it loomed over her in recurring nightmares. She half-expected to see the deer in front of it, the deer she had swerved to avoid when she caused the accident. She steadied herself on the hood of her father's car. Its smooth black surface was cool and comforting to her touch. She exhaled. The rock was beautiful in the fading light of the evening. Enid had almost forgotten how much later it got darker this far north. The tawny prairie grass was dancing behind the rock. Although this was the same view that Enid had seen in her recurring nightmares for more than twenty years, it did not frighten her this time.

"We are returning to the scenes of our crimes, Enid," said Atticus, wryly. It was this wry voice, so characteristic of her father, which had led to the success of his true crime podcast, *Murder on the High Plains*, which had paid for the Escalade, among other things. He told stories of his long career in crime reporting with an understated detachment and dry humour that audiences loved, particularly in the UK and Australia.

"You knew it was me driving, then?" Enid asked. "And you threw the police off the trail?"

"Of course." Sometimes the imperative is to survive. Look, you exist because of a problematic thing, overlaid on a problematic thing. I met your mother because I fled to Canada to escape the draft. And I crossed at the border crossing we are heading for. I haven't been back into the U.S since." He took a drag on his cigarette. "And dodging the draft, that's problematic, Enid. I didn't want to fight an unjust war, but I had to give up loyalty to my country to do it."

"People don't always do that, return to the scene of their crimes." Enid said. "When I was a prosecutor, it wasn't reliably true that they would return to the scene of their crimes. But sometimes they would."

"Yeah, they do it for lots of reasons. People return to scenes of crimes where passion was involved," Atticus said. "There are those that savour it. If you're a really sick fuck, you want to relive your misdeeds. Or sometimes people return to crime scenes to figure out what evidence is left there, to try not to get caught."

"Or maybe to try to get caught," Enid said, thinking that she had wished for an opportunity to plead guilty, to be absolved, or do penance. "Sometimes people want to be caught."

Atticus glanced at her. "Or they think they do."

"To get caught," Enid said, "so we can do some kind of penance, so we can pay what we owe."

"Penance! As though penance can ever really be enough. We can never pay what we owe," said Atticus. "Life is too big of a gift. Just do what you can where you can, Enid. You are here to survive. And then enjoy life. Maybe we are supposed to enjoy it."

"But Bruno... " Enid started.

"Old Bruno was dealing a lot of drugs back then, Enid. You don't know half of it. I gave the cops the story they wanted. It was a good story."

"Is it less of a good story if it isn't quite true?" Enid asked.

"There you go," said Atticus, with a playful glint in his eye, "confusing truth and fact. I gave them a true story. He was involved in serious amounts of drug dealing. And violence. You were a little girl, mixed up with him because you were on your own. I just omitted a couple of facts."

Enid shook her head. "In a court of law, the search for truth flows from the facts. The judge makes findings of fact and establishes the narrative of what happened on that basis, as you know."

"Enid," said Atticus, "they're not the same thing in literature. Careful fiction can tell us truths the facts cannot reveal, or at least not as clearly."

"I was a young woman, Dad. Not a little girl. I wanted to have a choice in it. I wanted to decide."

Atticus didn't reply for a long time. At last he said, "That's fair Enid. That's fair... We all make mistakes." He paused. "people return to the scenes of crimes for psychological reasons, they say. To get back on the horse that threw you. For traumatic re-enactment, to resolve it, because you're stuck there. To get unstuck. To master that horse at last."

"Dad, I was stuck there for a long time. Hiding from it. But not anymore. Not since I left Arthur."

"Yeah, yeah, that makes sense. You have to face it and own it to resolve it."

"I was hiding for too long, but the hiding place got confining."

"A second problematic thing of course is the background to all of this. It is colonialism, right?" asked Atticus. Here we are on Blackfoot land, going to prevail on the Blackfeet of Montana for mercy in the form of a vaccine."

"It is ironic," answered Enid.

"It is gracious. Sometimes people are, and sometimes life is, remarkably gracious. Trust it more, Enid. It's a lot of things. One of the things it is, is beautiful. Now, we are going to drive down there, and you are going to survive." He dropped his cigarette on the gravel. "You drive."

"You are going to let me drive the Caddy?" Enid laughed nervously, "Right down the road where I crashed a car and nearly killed two people?"

"You are going to get us there safely." He stepped decisively into the passenger seat.

Enid felt dizzy for a moment. She leaned over the car. There was a thud as something hit the ground. She looked up, thinking it must have been a rock. When she got back in the car, Enid was surprised to see that only about ten minutes had passed. Their conversation had been short but important.

They carried on down Highway 2, stopping at a Tim Hortons on the south side of the city to pick up some donuts for breakfast to go with the mandarins Atticus had in the car. They also stopped for dinner and arrived at the Piegan-Carway border crossing at 9:00p.m. There were a few white buildings standing against a rolling prairie backdrop under the big, dark, starry Alberta sky. The brown "Welcome to Alberta" sign stood on the other side of the road against a backdrop of rolling grasslands to the east and Glacier National Park's snow-covered peaks to the west.

Foremost among the peaks was Chief Mountain.

Atticus gestured at the peak. "It's called Ninaistako in the Blackfoot language and King's Peak by early European colonizers. The word 'Ninaistako' means great chief."

Arriving at the border, they ate the food picked up earlier from a Tim Hortons drive thru. This was where the Blackfeet tribe of Montana said it would give out surplus COVID-19 vaccines, not just to its First Nations relatives but to others, to anyone who made it. They hunkered down for the night.

The next day was a cloudy spring day. They awoke under the big Alberta sky amid the rolling hills where the green was just starting; the tawny grass waved in the wind like an ocean of straw. Oil derricks nodded here and there on the landscape, pumping the oil from ancient dinosaur bones into the wallets of Albertans. Atticus, a man of written words, said little. He was listening to Bob Dylan in the car.

Customs officials waved the line of cars across the border. Atticus steered his Escalade into the lineup behind hundreds of other cars on the Canadian side of the Alberta-Montana border. Directly in front of them was a red Ford pickup truck and behind them, a white minivan.

One by one, the vehicles from north of the border crossed into the US, going through a loop that took them through the vaccination facility and back across. When it came time for Enid and Atticus's turn, they showed their passports to a tired looking but rather disconcertingly handsome customs official whose name tag said Officer Andrews. Enid paused a moment, flustered. He smiled and said, "All good. You're free to go." He then waved them through the gate across the border, where they were ushered to a table and chairs sitting outside in the field.

The Indigenous nurses recited a prayer in the Blackfoot language before they began administering shots. Chief Mountain, sacred to the Blackfoot people, rose in the distance. Chief Mountain was a royal tower of rock, the same rock that formed the Okotoks rock, but coalesced and composed into a pile, into a community.

"What did the prayer mean?" asked Atticus of the nurse when it came time for his shot, always the interviewer. "What did the prayer mean, Miss? I'm a reporter." He was holding a spiral bound notebook.

"Miss?" laughed the woman. "It's Chogan. That's my name. In our language, it means blackbird. The prayer was to protect all of you people, and others, seeking refuge from the COVID-19 virus." Her smooth black hair was pulled back into a shiny bun that gleamed through the plastic cap she wore with her personal protective equipment. Her eyes danced about her mask. "You are looking for the story? Here it is. More than 95 per cent of our Blackfeet reservation's ten thousand people are fully immunized. We got vaccine allotments from the Montana Health Department and then also from the federal Indian Health Service. We got too many. They have expiration dates. We decided to help the other nations in the Blackfoot Confederacy, the three tribes in southern Alberta that share language and culture with us. And then we decided to help everyone we could. The solution is herd immunity. The solution for each of us is immunity for all of us. We must take care of each other. That's the medicine."

Enid sat down on a folding chair. She could see the outline of the Rockies in the distance and Chief Mountain prominently nearby. Even though it was April, snow mingled with the prairie grasses. The wind was blowing hard, whipping her hair around. Such a small poke from the needle, and it was done.

"Thank you," she said to Chogan, feeling overwhelmed by the moment and by the weight of history, of colonialism, and the incredible disproportionate kindness of this sharing of vaccines.

"Are you excited?" Chogan asked Enid.

"Yes, it's like the moon landing."

"It is," said the nurse. She looked up from the syringe, "It really is."

"Thank you," Enid said, suddenly crying. It was a turning point, a critical juncture, that puncture. She handed Chogan a bottle of Ouzo from Greece.

"Thank you," said the nurse, smiling brightly. She touched Enid's shoulder gently as Enid quivered with sobs. "In return, I have some good news, reporter man," she said, glancing at Atticus, who was sitting beside Enid, getting his vaccine.

"See that peak, the one they call Chief Mountain? We call it Ninaistako. The mountain is sacred. Indigenous people from all over North America travel to the base of the mountain, not now of course, because of COVID-19, but in a normal year, for sweet grass ceremonies, to place prayer flags and to perform religious rituals. That mountain, they say, will signal the end of the world. Our elders say that when it comes to the end of days, a great white god will appear from the top of Chief Mountain. When he departs from the mountain, it will crumble and be destroyed." Chogan smiled. "Look at the mountain. It's still standing. This is not." She laughed and winked. "The end of the world. And none of you white folks are gods."

Enid smiled back. Her heart was full. She was so grateful for the vaccine and for this time with her father. They returned to the car and sat the required fifteen minutes. Enid was still crying.

Of course, amid the tears, she had the presence of mind to post the vaccine selfie on Facebook, with the caption "Vaccinated Madafakas!" Enid's friends remarked that her social media presence, once carefully curated to be steeped in golden hour perfection, had changed. Enid had to own that, to own her contribution to the ironic hashtag #authenticity her marriage to Arthur had been.

Like the other Canadian vehicles whose occupants got the vaccines, Atticus's Escalade followed the loop they were directed to and immediately returned home. They were not allowed to linger on Blackfeet land or in the United States. They returned home with letters from health officials exempting them from the mandatory fourteen-day quarantine imposed on all those entering the country.

Enid said to Atticus on the road back to Calgary. "Canada has lagged in vaccinating our population because we weren't ruthless enough. We waited politely."

Atticus shook his head. "It's a practical problem. We lack the ability to manufacture the vaccine ourselves, so we had to rely on the global supply chain."

"Exactly," Enid said. "And we waited all this time, politely hiding in the basement because a wolf was outside. The Americans didn't hide, so they died in large numbers, but they shot the wolf. Canada hasn't been ruthless enough. You have to be ruthless to survive."

Atticus kept looking at her. "Maybe. But Canada is my country by choice. Precisely because it opted not to be as vicious as my home country did. Precisely because Canada stayed out of Vietnam. Ruthlessness has a value, yes, but so does discipline, so does compassion. We went to what they are calling the Medicine Line because the Blackfeet are being generous, not ruthless."

Enid was just grateful to be vaccinated. Enid Alger was going to survive.

The Rest

Atticus dropped Enid off at her mother's place on the way back. He didn't come inside, just waved from the window of his car, but he didn't wait for Enid's mother Judith to answer the door. He rolled up the glass window, and there was a wall between them again, reinstalled smoothly and quickly. Atticus had not magically become someone else, even with the passage of time. His car peeled away in a cloud of dust, and all that was left was the sound of a dog barking somewhere inside the trailer.

This was Enid's first visit to her mother's new home, on land west of Calgary, towards Cochrane, on rolling foothills overlooking the mountains. She now lived in a little white trailer with red trim. Outside, the grass was yellow, with patches of snow lingering in the shadowed areas. Judith later said the trailer itself was a Ruby Red 1956 Platt Camper. It was rounded and small, fifteen-feet in length, with two-toned white-and-red paint and chrome trim accents. It had matching wheels on its exterior.

Judith came to the door. Her long, curly red hair was tied back into a loose bun. She was a bit stooped now and looked smaller, but her blue eyes were as lively as ever. "Come in," she said excitedly, and gave Enid a tight hug, despite the pandemic and the passage of time since they had last seen each other. "I've been expecting you." Judith felt tiny but vigorous and wiry in Enid's arms. Inside, the tiny room smelled of freesia. The walls were shiny wood panelling. A black lab bounded up to Enid and wagged his tail. Judith laughed. "His name is Disco," she said.

"You seem so much better," Enid said to Judith, as she sipped chamomile tea from a peacock blue mug and Judith whirled around making a meal of biscuits and soup. Enid was seated on red and white tuck and roll vinyl upholstery on dinette cushions. The trailer had rear dinette seating reminiscent of a 1950s diner. It was a tiny space, but it felt capacious, and all of the nooks and crannies were used efficiently.

"I did a different sort of therapy," said Judith, the light of the evening illuminating her face through the trailer window. Dainty red curtains blew softly in the breeze where it was open a crack. "Finally. They called it EMDR [eye movement desensitization and reprocessing] therapy for PTSD. You revisit traumatic memories and process them. It was originally used for Vietnam vets. Atticus told me about it. He sent me news clippings in the mail." She gently stroked Disco's head as he sat beside her. "I agree. I am so much, so much better."

"Revisit traumatic memories?" Enid asked. "Like visiting an accident scene or like making peace with the past? Can we, can you ever make peace with the past?"

"Maybe not," said Judith. "Not peace exactly. But you can own it. You can face it. And you can move on from it."

"Like revisiting the scene of a crime."

Judith looked up at her. "I hadn't thought about it that way but maybe." She smiled. "I have been thinking quite a bit about crimes these days. I do tutoring at the Spy Hill jail. I end up talking to the men there as we practice reading. It's interesting and sad."

"That's really cool that you are doing that, Mom."

"Thanks – I love it. We've gone through *The Great Gatsby*, *The Catcher in the Rye*, *The Grapes of Wrath*, *The Colour Purple*, and *Ulysses*."

Enid cut her off. "Mom! Your banned book list!" Enid was laughing now. When Enid was a child, Judith had been fired from teaching at Calgary's public high schools for designing and delivering an English language arts curriculum based entirely on banned books. She had refused to teach what the Board required and had been relegated to substitute teaching and a low, precarious wage as a result.

"Yeah, those are the same banned books. I like it." Judith grinned. "And I encourage them to read other banned books, to question the rules, and to find a path forwards that way." She then turned more serious. "I have a sense of what it is like to be incarcerated, after all the time I spent in facilities. Not called the same thing but a lot of the same circumstances. Confinement. Hard to find hope."

Enid's lightheaded joy from that morning slid downhill into feverish chills and delirium by evening. "That vaccine hangover," Enid said to Elora via text message, "is very fucking real."

Judith said to Enid, as she sat on the dinette seat, "Stand up a second, sweetie. That transforms into a bed." And sure enough, with a few deft movements by Judith, the dinette seats became a king-size bed. "Tah Dah! And now I'm going outside." Enid hesitated, knowing it was her mother's bed, but she also felt exhausted and sickly. She lay there on the bed in the tiny room that was her mother's trailer, smelled the chamomile tea and freesia, heard her mother sing along to Van Morrison, and felt profoundly at peace. It was a respite she had craved for, since her mother had first been taken away to a mental hospital, rapidly, in the night, with no out-patient treatment options explored. It happened more than thirty or so years ago, before Enid had really grown up.

Enid checked her work email. There was a message from the Okotoks detachment of the Alberta Royal Canadian Mounted Police.

The email message read: "Your wallet has been found near the Okotoks rock. Please contact us."

The thudding sound! Must not have been a rock. Must have been her wallet. Enid phoned the number, apprehensive about what the officer might say about her clearly breaching interprovincial travel regulations and being present in Alberta.

"Officer," Enid said, "yes, that is my ID, and I travelled to Alberta. I was driving." Her heart was racing. It seemed that Arthur wouldn't even need to report her to authorities. She was caught.

"Oh good," said the woman police officer. "We were a bit concerned. It was located next to a dead deer. Your ID cards were strewn around where the body rested. At first, we thought it was the scene of a car accident, but there were no marks of an impact on the deer. This beautiful old stag. Very strange."

"Yes," Enid said, catching her breath. "Strange indeed."

"We will mail the ID back to your Ottawa address. Stay safe, Mrs. Kimble."

"Thank you. It's Enid Alger, actually officer. I'm recently divorced."

"I'm sorry," the officer said.

"Don't be. I'm not."

Enid Kimble—hypocritical social media maven who worked tirelessly to inspire the envy of her childhood friends, bulimic food blogger, closet smoker, decorator of suburban homes and maker of plans, occasional shoplifter, wife to the prestigious surgeon Dr. Arthur Kimble, half of a power couple—had been lost in the COVID-19 pandemic. When, as a couple, they had scraped off the trappings of wealth and travel as well as the thin veneer of shallow socializing, when the cocktail parties ended and the airports emptied, when the pandemic dismantled the platform for their power couple presentation, when there was no longer a stage to perform their show of suburban bliss, there was nothing holding Enid and Arthur together. There was no backstage rapport.

Enid lay on the couch in her mother's trailer listening to Judith sing while puttering around the garden outside with Disco. She then called her friend Elora.

"Survived so far," she said.

"Good. Expected," said Elora. The conversation ended there.

Enid felt the room spinning around her, and her cheeks were flushed with fever.

"Mom, I need to go home, to my kids."

"Tomorrow," said Judith, "Enid, you are having a vaccine reaction. You have to rest. You can't help them unless you rest first. Rest." She put her cool hand on Enid's forehead, as Enid had wished she had been there to do long ago when Judith had been in the mental institution and Enid was a teen, alone, in their house.

Enid lay down on the couch and listened to the sound of the wind, the wind chimes, the birds, and Judith singing as she walked around the garden with Disco.

She group facetimed her kids

"I got vaxxed, kiddos, Booyah," she said.

"Whatevs, Mom. I'd be more excited if it was me," Freya said.

"Does that mean we can get to Harry Potter World sooner?" Wolfgang asked.

"Soon as they open the border, baby. And I will find a way to get you guys vaccinated as soon as I can."

"Are you on a bus, Mom?" Morgana asked.

"No, honey, this is Nana's house. It's a trailer. It's really cool."

"Okay mom," Sybil said.

"How's Nana?" Morgana asked.

"Good," Enid said. "Really good. Can't wait for you guys to see her."

"Who's that?" a voice said in the background behind Sybil. Arthur appeared behind her head on the screen. He was wearing his scrubs. Bags were very visible below his eyes.

"Oh, I see. Enid."

"Arthur," Enid said. "You look tired."

"Sorry about your face too, Enid," said Arthur.

Enid laughed. "You haven't called the po-po on me yet, I guess?"

"No," said Arthur. "I have not yet reported your reckless, redemptive, narcissistic road trip despite your flagrant disregard of the laws of several jurisdictions."

"Well," Enid said, "I guess thanks for holding in your fascist impulses temporarily. I guess the question is really what constitutes essential travel. What, really, is essential?"

"Oh gawd Enid," said Arthur, "I have officially withdrawn from your philosophy and mythology lessons. Enough."

Enid sighed, blinking back tears, because Arthur could still hurt her. "Anyway, po-po know, dude. They already know and surprisingly enough they have other stuff to do other than bother me. But, in all seriousness, thanks for being with the kids."

"They are my kids, Enid."

"I know. Thank you," she was crying openly now, "for them. For taking care of them."

As usual, emotion had a reverse magnetism on Arthur. With a swift, abrupt flash of green from his scrubs, Arthur exited stage left and was off screen.

"K mom," Sybil said. "Gotta go. Loves you."

"Loves you babies."

"Loves you, ho bag." Sybil said.

Enid lay down on the trailer bed with her eyes closed and let the tears fall across her cheeks. She must have fallen asleep because, when she phoned her friend Elora, her voice sounded scratchy. Enid realized that, by now, it was late in Ontario.

"Elora," she said, "I love the feeling of a vaccine hangover. Best reason to feel like an ass I could imagine."

"Fan-fucking-tastic, my friend," shouted Elora. "And I won my case today, the one I told you about!"

"Girl got acquitted for the reckless driving charge?"

"Fuck yes!" said Elora. "No plea deal. The judge tore the Crown a new one."

"Congratulations! That's awesome!"

"Thanks. It was a fucking trip. Loved it. Girl got to walk away. I hope she can do some fucking fabulous stuff with her life, move on up from child welfare to something amazing. You never know."

"You never know. So great! Maybe she will be prime minister. I'm not even kidding. Everyone deserves a fighting chance. Maybe she will also find love out there... I think I'm going to get a boyfriend. Try my hand at love."

"Jesus, Enid, do you have fucking delirium? You were married for a long time. Try being single. Try being yourself. Figure out who that is. There will always be some random dude willing to fuck you, if that's what you are worried about. Men are simple folk. They don't like women, Enid. They like pussies."

"Elora, I love you but that's harsh even for you. That's not it," Enid said. "I'm thinking about Aristotle and his idea that people are half-souls split apart and have to find their complementary piece. I don't know if there are soul mates. I just know Arthur wasn't mine."

"I'm thinking about Aristotle," Elora repeated in a high-pitched, mocking voice. "Stop! That's the fever talking, my friend. And if it's not the fever, get a dose of reality. You've been watching too many rom coms. Aristotle Shmaristotle. You are complete already."

"Maybe. But maybe it's worth a shot."

"Soul mate troll bait," said Elora. "Bruh!"

Enid laughed. "You sound like my kids. When did you go all Gen Z on me, Elora?" And then she said, more seriously, "I don't want to die alone. I don't want to end up alone. I'm scared of that."

"I get that. But are you alone right now, Enid? Am I alone? We are talking to each other. I hear your mom singing terribly in the background. It is epically bad. There's no fucking way that's a recording. Pretty sure that murderous travesty to Van Morrison was the soundtrack to your coming into the world too. You weren't born alone. Judith was there with you. And you're not alone now. You've got your kids. You've got friends— like me."

"Remember L. M. Montgomery?" Enid asked, brightening. "And *Anne of Green Gables*? She always talked about kindred spirits."

"Do I? Fuck yes! Gilbert Blythe. I would have banged him right out of the parochial nineteenth century and into the twentieth, nah the twenty-first. Eg-fucking-zactly Enid. I've got your back."

"Damn. Gilbert Blythe is probably why I married a doctor," Enid said, laughing, thinking wistfully about the long-lashed blue eyes of the handsome actor who had played him in the 1980s Canadian Broadcasting Corporation adaptations of the *Anne of Green Gables* books, Jonathan Crombie. "I was in the seventh grade, and he was my first love."

"And you didn't realize Arthur wasn't Gil. You mix fact and fiction Enid; you don't know the difference between them. That's it at the bottom of it. I'm not sure you can see my eye roll well enough because it's dark, bioyotch. Of course that L. M. Montgomery flowers and rainbows and soul mates in the garden shit is little Enid's version of porn. Probably you figured you were marrying Gil when you hooked up with the surgical psychopath."

"Hey, don't underestimate L. M. Montgomery. She has given a hundred years of Canadian girls inspiration to follow their ambitions and wear puffed sleeves. You may, however, have a point about Arthur. It was always difficult to figure out who he really was."

"Mkay, whatever you say, Enid. Arthur was always detached—with everybody. I hope he figures out how not to be that way with your kids. But that's on him. For you, in the meantime, here's a suggestion: Maybe don't make any more fucking life plans based on PG-rated TV shows. Disney is fiction. Anne of Green Gables is fiction. They're stories for crying to with ice cream; they are not super realistic. Soul mates sound like a waste of energy. Soul mates! Gag me with a fucking spoon! Look where this pie-eyed star-gazing shit got you! Carried away by your romantic visions. You had five kids in five years with Mr. minuscule fuckstick fucker Arthur, the surgical sociopath. Not a good work-life balance strategy. Not a good self-care strategy. Not a good fucking career plan."

"He's not a bona fide sociopath. Every once in a while, I see humanity come through. He's just a mess. Afraid, I think, that if he feels anything then everything will be too much. So he whitewashed all the walls in our old house and uses my books as décor items. Maybe he's right. Maybe that makes him happy. Maybe books hurt you more when you actually read them. Maybe he's just surviving. And I love them though, the kids, those teenage monsters."

"Yeah, I love your monsters too, little shits. And, whatever, Arthur's not anything particularly special. He's just some guy. He's a guy with a god complex, but he's really kind of average, run of the mill, garden-variety, conventional stuff. I'm not fucking around. You are a professional in your fucking prime. Show those monsters how it can be done! Write a good story, Enid. Give 'em a role model, not a weepy, mopey seventh grader in a middle-aged body! You are Enid fucking Alger, and you aced law school, and you rock a barrister's robe. Maybe the tabs on it are your soulmates. Maybe there is some dude out there. Maybe there is not, but so what. Maybe it's feminist Ryan Gosling come to life from the memes, holding an ice-cold prosecco and a fucking golden retriever puppy. Have some fun, but he's not the plot, my friend! Live your own fucking story. Don't sell yourself short."

"Elora Frank," Enid said. "Even in my weakened state, I recognize that was an epic pep talk. Almost like you know how to do persuasive advocacy. You are really, really fucking fantastic, you know that?"

"I know that. Travel safe my friend."

"Thanks," Enid said and hung up, falling asleep almost immediately, dreaming of dancing as Judith's fabulously terrible rendition of "Into the

Mystic" wafted in from outside. Enid's planned trip was not ever intended to be a journey from one man to another. It was Enid's journey into herself, cutting back the ruins, excavating, pulling back the detritus of all the years, to find solid ground on which to mindfully rebuild, to do what we have to do in order to create something new—to find a solid place to build on and pay attention to what we are making.

Enid Kimble did not make it through the COVID-19 pandemic.

Enid Alger, however, mother to many blessed and beautiful wild-hearted children, mythology fangirl, devotee of animals, both wild and tame, fierce lawyer, loving daughter of Atticus and Judith, barefoot child of Calgary's sparkling lights under a big prairie sky, would survive. It wouldn't be perfect, surviving, Enid knew, as she shivered in a cold sweat in her bed after the vaccine. The pandemic would wear on agonizingly slowly leaning towards its conclusion. It would hurt like hell. But it would be worth it. She would make plans and have to remake them, and she was not sure where she would be in five years, but she knew it would be worth it, knew she would be living from her heart, living with love, living amongst ruins as we all do, ruins where there would be hope for treasure. In the morning, her mother would drive her to the airport, and she would return to Ottawa to take care of her children and to live on in her life as a lawyer. She would rebuild.

Enid lay on the couch in her mother's trailer, waking up and falling asleep again, listening to Judith's marvellously loud and not particularly melodic voice bellowing along to Maren Morris's country twang boldly singing "My Church":

I've cussed on a Sunday

I've cheated, and I've lied

I've fallen down from grace

A few too many times

But I find holy redemption

When I put this car in drive

Roll the windows down and turn up the dial

Can I get a hallelujah

Can I get an amen

Feels like the Holy Ghost running through ya

When I play the highway FM

I find my soul revival

Singing every single verse

Yeah I guess that's my church

When Hank brings the sermon

And Cash leads the choir

It gets my cold, cold heart burning

Hotter than a ring of fire

When this wonderful world gets heavy

And I need to find my escape

I just keep the wheels rolling, radio scrolling

'Til my sins wash away.

June

It was in June—after the April snow had at last melted and Ottawa's tulips had come and gone in May, when the heat picked up in Ottawa during the reopening after a year of COVID-19 lockdowns—that Enid one day stopped wearing the bracelet. Sybil noticed, "Mom, you took off your weird ass bracelet from Daddy's ring."

Enid was sitting in her car with all five of her children. The girls were on the way to a cheerleading practice, and she was going to take Wolfgang to play tennis in the meantime.

"Yeah, that was a fugly bracelet," Morgana said.

"No, it wasn't ugly," Freya said. "Your face is ugly, Morgue."

"Hilarious, Freeka," Morgana said.

Enid looked at her bare wrist below her hands on the steering wheel of her Lincoln SUV, glancing to the right at Wolfgang sitting shotgun. Her teen girls were all glammed up by a spa visit, sitting in the back. They had their long, acrylic nails and their long highlighted hair, their false eyelashes, and militant GenZ Mom jeans. She wasn't always sure how to connect with her children. Wolfgang had asked her about how to shave. She wasn't sure how to help him.

"I just didn't need to wear it anymore," she said.

"What are you going to do with it?" Freya asked.

"I put it in my jewellery box. So you four can fight over it after I'm dead."

"What about me?" Wolfgang asked, facetiously. "You homophobic? Maybe I want a bracelet."

Enid rolled her eyes. "Okay, then, for the five of you to fight over while I'm in my coffin then."

"Bah," Morgana said. "We'll be dead before that from climate change."

They all laughed, and their laughter for a moment rang out like it had when they were little, brightening the corners of the car. Enid was warmed by it and could tell the kids were too. It was one of the magic moments, like when she and her Wolfgang had shot each other at laser tag, one of the nice family moments between her and her kids that were coming back into being. Enid liked thinking about that laughter as she listened to a song by Traveller, "Hummingbird", about being single after a long time, about online dating, and about Thelma and Louise getting away with it, instead of driving off a cliff. She liked it. Liked the idea of maybe not atoning, not doing penance, just going on, finding a way to be free, as free as possible, and living.

"Mom, I am reading Ibsen's *A Doll House* for class," Frey said. "It made me sad. It was interesting in parts, with her being a housewife and sad and wanting more, but mostly really boring, and sad that Nora had no path forwards, except for leaving at the end, even leaving her kids. Mom, it's about impossibility."

"I guess it's still true, what was true for Nora. You'll never win." Enid's hands tightened on the steering wheel. She felt her breath grow sharp as they stopped at a red light, realizing the truth of the statement as she said it. "You'll never win against patriarchy. We can't make a perfect ending, can't make a happy ever after; it's the double bind. We just have to do what makes sense for us. We'll never win against the way things are, the weight of expectations and hopes. They're a hulk; it's a wreck. The structures loom large around us. We just need to find the places where flowers can grow amid the ruins."

"Oh, fuck that, Mom," Morgana said, from the backseat, not looking up from Tiktok on her iPhone. "That's so cringe, just like a fake lawyer would say it. Don't tell us we can't win. Don't underestimate us."

The light turned green, and Enid accelerated. "Language aside, Morgana," she said, " I appreciate the sentiment." She glanced into the rear view mirror. "On the way back, Freya, how about if you drive?"

"Argh," Wolfgang said. "When Freyas are drivers, how will there be survivors?"

"She has to learn how. I'll help her. We will all be fine." Enid glanced down at her hands on the steering wheel. Many years ago, strong arms had pulled her from the wreckage of a horrific car crash and from her youthful recklessness and the torn threads of the family patterns into which she had been born. She was not on her way home to a mansion; her modest house was a far cry from a great kingdom, no Camelot of legend. But now when she looked down at the steering wheel, the strong arms that she knew she could rely upon to guide them all safely home were her own.

And, for once, with the comfortable banter between all of them, all five of Enid's children smiled at the same time.

Author's Note

This is, of course, a work of fiction. However, it engages with historical events and real places. The COVID-19 pandemic was, of course, very real. The Greek Islands are as described. You should go. Grail Springs is a real place, near Bancroft, Ontario. Go there too. Enid's home city of Ottawa is Canada's quaint and iconic capital, made famous by anti-vaccine riots in 2022, a sleepy government town that became the global epi-centre of controversy around pandemic lockdown measures. It's gorgeous. You should visit.

This story is about reconciliation and ruinous kingdoms in the personal but also in a broader sense. In April 2021, the Montana Blackfeet really did undertake a nation-to-nation act of reconciliation by offering vaccin-ations to their Canadian neighbours along what was known as the Med-icine Line. In writing this story, where Alberta's land is such an important feature, it is crucial for me to acknowledge that what we now call Alberta is the traditional and ancestral territory of many peoples, presently subject to Treaties 6, 7, and 8: the Blackfoot Confederacy— Kainai, Piikani, and Siksika—the Cree, Dene, Saulteaux, Nakota Sioux, Stoney Nakoda, the Tsuu T'ina Nation, and the Métis people of Alberta. This includes the Métis settlements and the six regions of the Métis Nation of Alberta within the historical Northwest Metis Homeland. I acknowledge the many First Nations, Métis, and Inuit who have lived in and cared for these lands for generations. I am grateful for the traditional Knowledge Keepers and Elders who are still with us today and those who have gone before us. I make this acknowledgement as an act of reconciliation and gratitude to those whose territory this story travels.

Everything else in this story flows from my imagination.

I am grateful for the support of many people who made this book possible. First, I owe a great debt of gratitude to my patient and wonderful editor, Christine Peets, who deserves full credit for the idea of writing this second book about Enid and finishing her story. Thank you, as always, to Andrea O'Reilly for her magnificent work in feminist publishing in making this book possible. Thank you also to my friends and family. There are so many of you I am blessed to have in my life. Thank you. Special thanks to Izabela MacDougall, Elana Finestone, Katharine Caza, Jannene Bancroft, Nonavee Dale, Kate Terroux, Laura Farley Ratcliffe, Sarah Mackenzie, Deborah Mervitz, Amanda Davis, and the inimitable Bevin Worton, among others. Props also to Cindy Almond for her wizardry in travel planning and to the Klahoose Nation, on whose lands this novel was completed. Thanks to Barbara Diaz, who helps me find my feet. Last but not least thanks to Carolynn Campbell, who knows how to talk to mermaids.

Most importantly: So much love to my children: Helaina, Andromeda, Myrina, and Desmond. Your smiles are my happily ever after.